T0209234

Dreams and Wishes, Wishes and Dreams

THEDA YAGER

WESTBOW
PRESS*
A DIVISION OF THOMAS NELSON
& ZONDERVAN

WestBow Press books may be ordered through booksellers or by contacting:

WestBow Press
A Division of Thomas Nelson & Zondervan
1663 Liberty Drive
Bloomington, IN 47403
www.westbowpress.com
1 (866) 928-1240

ISBN: 978-1-5127-9247-8 (sc)
ISBN: 978-1-5127-9248-5 (hc)
ISBN: 978-1-5127-9246-1 (e)

Library of Congress Control Number: 2017910374

Print information available on the last page.

WestBow Press rev. date: 07/05/2017

Dreams and Wishes, Wishes and Dreams is dedicated to every child or young person who has struggled to achieve his or her goal in life.

To those youth, I say hold on to your dreams.

The journey may be long and difficult, but the prize of success awaits you.

Work hard. Hold on to your dream and make it happen.

You can do it.

I wish you much success in all you do.

A big thank you to my husband, Don Yager, of sixty years, for reading and editing my manuscript. Another thank you to Amber Clark for making suggestions of neighborhoods where med students might have found housing.

Chapter 1

❖❖❖

This story began in the late 1960s. There was a small town in southern America with medium-sized mountains and beautiful, clear streams of water running along the valleys. This story happened before cell phones and personal computers existed. Communication wasn't as easy and fast as today. The United States Postal Service delivered mail to each house. The mailman knew each family—and in some cases, all the family news and gossip.

Generally, there were one or two phones in the house: one hanging on the wall in the kitchen, attached to a very long cord, and maybe a second one in the parents' bedroom. Long-distance phone calls were charged by the minute. Most modest, little homes had one TV, which was generally a large piece of bulky furniture located in the living room. To change channels, you had to get out of your comfortable chair, walk across the room, and turn a knob to select a show from one of only three channels.

The neighborhood where this story takes place was in a blue-collar community. It was a small, stable community made up of hardworking people; in some homes, both husband and wife worked to make ends meet. The number one place of employment was the garment industry. Generations of families had enjoyed living in the area. The main interests for the parents centered on school activities for their children, hometown parades, Fourth of July fireworks, and Christmas celebrations. Neighborhoods were stable. Each little home had two or three bedrooms and one or two baths, and it was approximately nine hundred to twelve hundred square feet in size. Honeymooners would move into a home, raise their families, and live out their entire lives in one neighborhood.

In one such house lived Charlene Jamison. Next door was a boy named James Walters, whose daddy had built a large tree house in the backyard. The two families had been friends ever since they moved to Wilsonville, Alabama. Charlene and James had been friends since infancy. The children attended kindergarten through eighth grade together. They had been best friends always. They played, laughed, cried, fought, wrestled, and made up almost like brothers and sisters would do. Neither made a decision without talking with his or her best buddy.

In those days, children could move freely in the neighborhood. Most homes had stay-at-home moms, who were always watching out for the neighborhood children. Adults everywhere watched for large swarms of bicycles moving from house to house. You could generally tell where the neighborhood kids were playing by the large pile of bicycles in the front yards.

Life continued with much the same day-to-day living until one fateful day. Charlene's dad came home and said the plant was closing. He would be losing his job. For now, Charlene's mother's job appeared secure at another business.

James's and Charlene's dads worked for the same business. Both men were talking about moving to another city or state to find employment. Charlene's dad said he would come home when he could, if he could find work close by.

People began trying to sell their homes. But who would buy them? Who would want to move to a town where the number one industry had been sold to an overseas firm with the plant moving to another country?

The closing sent shock waves through the small town. Teachers were talking about the impact this would have on schools. The county and city offices were stressed because they were losing tax revenue. No one in the town was unaffected.

Money became very tight. Banks wouldn't lend money. They were even calling in loans to be paid at once. Tempers became short, and home life in the once idyllic community was now in turmoil. Fathers began to drink heavily, though money was limited. Too often police were called to homes because of spousal abuse.

As the adult world was crumbling around them, children huddled together to draw comfort from one another. They were hesitant to ask their parents for money for school supplies because when requests were made, they received a lecture about the wasting and scarcity of money.

Soon families boarded up their homes and left town. A few lingered on, primarily because they had no place to move to.

James's parents were preparing to move to another state. Charlene's dad had left town to go to another city to find work.

Charlene and James huddled together to discuss what was happening and what would happen when he moved away. The young friends had never been apart in their lives. They shared secrets, wishes, hopes, and dreams. At school, they competed in everything.

Now, they were to be separated.

One summer's evening, the two youngsters sat on the front lawn, looking up at the stars. James said, "Every night at eight o'clock, I will look at the Big Dipper and think about you. Promise me that you will work hard in school, and I promise you the same. When we're twenty-one, promise me you will meet me back here in Wilsonville at the City Park on the Fourth of July. I will look for you in the gazebo. I'll write to you when I can get postage stamps. I'll work hard, too. I promise. Will you please promise to think of me at eight o'clock each night? Find the Big Dipper if you can, look at it, and think of me."

Times were different in the 1960s and well into the early 1980s. Cell phones and private computers weren't available to make communication easy and fast.

Charlene sat, sobbing. Her best friend was moving away forever. Her dad had gone to a big city to find work. It would be just her and her mother left in Wilsonville. What would she do? How could they make it alone?

James put his arm around her shoulder and tried to comfort her, even though his heart was breaking too.

James and his parents were leaving town. They had been packing all day and planned to leave early the next morning. There were things they couldn't take, so they gave them to Charlene's mother.

The next morning, after a fitful night's sleep, the two households woke early, dreading what the next day would hold for them. Neighbors who hadn't left town lined the street, waving and crying as James and his parents drove down the street. Charlene stood in the street, crying and waving so long as she could see the moving truck. Her mother put her arms around her and held her tight. She was also crying. James's mother was her best friend. She told Charlene, "We will get through these hard times, and we'll be stronger because of them."

With heavy hearts, the remaining neighbors wearily walked back to their homes, wondering who would be next to move from this once-busy and happy street. Wilsonville had already lost more than a third of its population. Daily, it seemed, moving trucks, loaded pickups, and cars pulled out of driveways. Families hoped to find elsewhere what they had once enjoyed in this little town.

Charlene's dad had been gone two weeks when the mail carrier brought a letter, saying he had found a job. It wasn't in the garment industry, but it was a job. He was working on an offshore oil rig out in the Gulf of Mexico. He would be making good money and would work two weeks and then be off a week. He would really like his family to move to Houston as soon as the house was sold. He sent Charlene's mother a check to help pay the bills.

Soon a new normal was taking place in Wilsonville. The people who remained grew closer together. They helped one another and volunteered for projects around town that had once been salaried jobs. By keeping the town looking nice, they weren't as depressed as they had been before. They even cut the grass around vacant houses.

Charlene's mother kept working her job and tried to keep home life as normal as possible for her daughter.

During the summer months, Charlene spent a lot of time in the library. She read books about faraway places. She read about other cultures and how other people lived. She visited her pastor and volunteered to help with little jobs around the church.

One day, Pastor Jones asked her whether she would like to visit a child in the hospital. The child was very sick and had been in the hospital for long periods of time. The community had held bake sales and garage sales to help raise money to pay the mounting hospital bills.

When Charlene met the child, she saw an eight-year-old boy who was so frail and weak that he couldn't walk. Charlene asked him whether it would be all right if she brought some books and read with him. He liked that idea. He told her he liked race cars, sports, and exciting things. She promised she would go to the library and look for books he might enjoy.

All summer, Charlene made time to visit her new little friend, Peter. She soon forgot how sad she was and began to look forward to visiting Peter. Soon he was reading some of the books to Charlene. They enjoyed these special times.

It wasn't long until school would be starting again. Charlene dreaded high school because James wouldn't be there. Each time she walked up to her home, she automatically looked over at the boarded-up house where he had once lived. Each night at eight o'clock, she sat on the lawn, looked for the Big Dipper, and thought about James.

One day when she came home from school, her mother said, "Charlene, I have a surprise for you."

Curious, Charlene went to her. "Is Daddy coming home?"

Her mother answered, "No, I have a letter for you." Heart racing, Charlene eagerly took the letter from her mother's hand. It was from James.

Charlene ripped the letter open and began to read aloud.

Dear Charlene,

We are in Idaho. Dad has a job working on a large horse ranch. I wish you could see this country! The trees and mountains are so tall, and the lakes and streams of water are unbelievably clear. We understand it gets very cold in the winter. I must tell you about that when winter gets here.

And the stars are very bright. We have a clear view of the Big Dipper. On a clear night, it stands out brightly against a dark sky. I think of you when I see it. Please write to me and tell me what all has happened since we moved away.

Your friend always,
James

Dancing around the room with peals of giggles and laughter, all the while clapping her hands, Charlene said, "James wrote to me! He really, really did. I was afraid he had forgotten all about me." She dashed out of the room and ran to her bedroom to write a letter to him. She would have it in tomorrow's mail.

In her letter, she said,

Dear James,

Daddy has a job on an offshore drilling rig in the Gulf of Mexico. He works two weeks and has a week off. When he is not working, he lives in Houston. He wants us to move there as soon as the house sells. But houses are not selling. Mother still has her job. Daddy sends us money to help pay the bills. More people have moved since you left town. Wilsonville's population is getting very small.

School starts in two weeks. I am dreading starting high school without you there. I felt as if you were my big brother, always looking out for me. I don't know how I can do this. You have always been there from kindergarten on. I have been going to the library and doing a lot of reading about faraway places and various people who live different lives from ours. And I have been helping Pastor Jones with some chores at church, and he invited me to visit a little boy by the name of Peter, who has been in the hospital a very long time.

I like little Peter. I read to him each afternoon. The town has held garage sales and bake sales, raising money to help with his hospital bills. When I am reading to him and making him laugh, I forget how much I miss you. But, as soon as I go home, I can't help but look across at your house, still expecting to see you on the porch. I miss you. Write again soon.

Your friend always,
Charlene

The days sped by, and it was time for school to resume. The classes were very small, and there were fewer teachers. Some teachers were teaching two or more subjects. Times were hard for everyone.

Charlene saw some of the kids she had known through the years. They hadn't been close friends. Nonetheless, they were happy to see each other. All of them were still sad about what had happened in their community. They discussed friends who had moved away. And in the backs of their minds, they wondered when the moving truck would pull into their own driveways.

She worked very hard in all her classes, making good grades. She was determined to keep the promise she had made to James.

Their letters continued to be exchanged once or twice a week. It was exciting to hear about the beautiful place where James lived. He told her about the horses he and his dad worked with. He also said he liked his high school. It was much larger than the one back in Wilsonville. Things were going well for his family, but they were still homesick.

Charlene's mother would hear from her husband once or twice a week. Initially he wrote his family often. Then the letters began to taper off. They might hear from him once or twice a month. Then the letters were brief and impersonal. Charlene's mother asked him to please come home on the weeks when he wasn't working.

Weeks and months continued to speed past. Christmas season arrived. A letter arrived from Charlene's father. She was so happy to get the letter from the mailbox. She was just sure he would say he was coming home for Christmas. Her mother ripped open the letter with happy anticipation. Then her hand went to her shocked and colorless face. Tears began to spill down her cheeks. His letter read,

> Dear Margaret and Charlene,
>
> This is a hard letter to write to you, but I must. You see, I have met someone else and want a divorce. I want to make my home here and do not plan to ever go back to Wilsonville. You will be hearing from my lawyer. If you can sell the house, then you can have whatever you get out of it. I will have that written in the divorce decree. I just want my freedom, and I want to move on with my life with the woman I love. You will hear from my lawyer soon.
>
> George

Margaret and Charlene collapsed into each other's arms, weeping uncontrollably. Their hopes and dreams for a happy Christmastime together as a family had been dashed in one short letter.

Charlene looked at her mother's tear-stained face and said, "Mother, we will get through this, and we will be stronger despite it."

Another sleepless night was ahead for both, with tear-stained pillows.

When Charlene went to her bedroom, she wrote a letter to James.

> Dear James,
>
> Mother and I had hoped Daddy would be home for Christmas. But that is not the case. We received a letter today, saying my daddy has met someone else and wants a divorce. Mother is just devastated. I am not sure what we will do or how we will manage. Please ask your parents to pray for us.
>
> Your friend always,
> Charlene

True to her father's word, in a few weeks, divorce papers were delivered to the home. Now the process of all the legal business would begin.

A letter arrived from James, and it couldn't have come at a better time. Margaret and Charlene needed to hear about someone else's life and for a few minutes not think about their own sorrow.

Dear Charlene,

Sometime back I said I would tell you about wintertime in northern Idaho. Are you seated? Some extreme temperatures have been recorded at minus-sixty degrees, but minus twenty or minus thirty is common. So far, we have had two feet of snow with high winds and more snow expected. The high winds cause snow to drift, making it very hard to get to where the cattle and horses are located to feed them. Daddy and the foreman used a snowplow on the truck to clear a path for trucks carrying hay and feed to their pens and shelters.

Some of the ranchers couldn't get to their cattle and horses to feed them and had to have hay airlifted in and dropped from airplanes. Next time you say, "Brrrrr, it is cold!" stop and think about this. But school is seldom canceled in town because snowplows keep the roads clear.

We have been using a snowplow on the front of a tractor to keep our driveway cleared out to the highway. I wish you could see the snow drifts. The wind blows the snow against the sides of hills, making beautiful swirls and designs.

Rivers freeze over. Later on, I will tell you what it is like when the spring thaw comes and the river breaks up. I understand it is an amazing thing to see. Well, maybe I should have said I will tell you if I remember to tell you.

The old-timers tell us to put up sheets of plywood on the outside of the house, covering all large ground-level windows. The snow can get so deep and heavy that it can break through the windows, and then it can come crashing into the house if the windows aren't covered. That is during the years when there is a heavy snowfall. Now, didn't I tell you more about wintertime in Idaho than you ever wanted to know?

Your friend always,
James

Charlene went to church and spoke with Pastor Jones about her daddy's divorcing her mother because he had met another woman. She looked at the pastor, and it seemed there were lines in his face she had never seen before. And his hair—was it turning gray? At that moment, she realized he had heard heartbreaking stories from all the members in the congregation. She felt guilty for having shared the problem her family was experiencing. She felt guilty for asking her mother for school supplies, even for a new pair of shoes, and certainly for a special treat or present.

She asked the pastor, "Do you know anyplace in town where I could get a job and help my mother with expenses?"

He looked at her with tender, grief-filled eyes and saw yet another one of the young people putting childhood behind and stepping into the adult world. He suggested, "Try applying for work at grocery stores, the drugstore, restaurants, and even at the hospital where you have been reading to Peter. Many of the part-time jobs are taken by adults who are working two jobs and just trying to survive the financial crisis that has struck Wilsonville. Also, if you are not afraid of working for a very precise but compassionate lady, Mrs. Samuelson is looking for a housekeeper. You could talk with her and ask her exactly what she has in mind. Explain to her your situation and be sure to tell her you are in high school. Be up front and honest with her and explain which days of the week and the times you can help her. I think you will find her to be a very understanding lady."

Charlene asked, "Is there anything I can volunteer to help with around the church? I don't want to receive pay. I just want to help you and our congregation."

He answered, "No, but I will keep your offer in mind if something comes up. Wherever you find a job, do not neglect your schoolwork. This hard place in your life will pass. You will move on with life, but you need an education to move on. Please don't neglect your studies."

Just before she left his study, she said, "One more thing. James and his parents are living in Idaho. His father is working on a horse ranch. They are homesick but doing well. James likes the high school. Thank you, Pastor Jones, for your suggestions."

Leaving the pastor's office, Charlene walked over to Mrs. Samuelson's home. It was a very large Victorian style home with a beautiful, wide porch with large, white posts and ornate trim. It looked like something out of a picture book, certainly not like Charlene's side of town. Hesitantly, Charlene rang the doorbell.

Soon Mrs. Samuelson answered the door. "Young lady, may I help you?"

Charlene introduced herself and said, "I have been in Pastor Jones's office, and he mentioned that you might need someone to help with housework. I am a high school student and would like to talk with you about that position if this is a convenient time. If it isn't, maybe I can make an appointment."

Mrs. Samuelson's jolly face broke into a smile, and she said, "Child, please come in. Pastor Jones called and said you were coming. Come in and tell me about yourself. Would you like something cold to drink? A Coke? Iced tea? Let's sit in the kitchen. It is my favorite room in the house."

At once Charlene began to relax. She liked Mrs. Samuelson immediately. Soon they were talking as if they had always been best friends. Mrs. Samuelson asked Charlene about school. What subjects did she really like?

Instantly Charlene responded, "I like all my classes and am making good grades in everything, but I especially *love* math and science classes.

"I am taking algebra and biology now. Next will be upper-level math and science classes. I've talked with the guidance counselor, and she has laid out an educational plan for me that should prepare me for college."

Mrs. Samuelson asked, "Do you have a boyfriend?"

Charlene said, "No, I had a very special friend, whom I had known since we were babies. He was my best friend, but he and his family moved to Idaho. I am so busy. I do not have time to think about dating right now. No, there is no one I am interested in dating that shares my interests."

Again, Mrs. Samuelson chuckled. She sat for a moment, sipping iced tea, and then said, "There is plenty of time for dating. You get your education, and the rest will fall into place."

Then she asked about Charlene's parents.

Charlene said her mother was working in town and that her father had lost his job along with many others when the garment factory moved overseas. As a matter of fact, she said, "Daddy got a job on an offshore oil rig in the Gulf of Mexico. He lives in Houston. For a while he sent us money each month to help pay the bills, but now he has stopped doing that. Some weeks ago, mother and I received a letter from him, saying he wanted to divorce my mother because he has met another woman and wants to start life anew. Mother and I had planned to move to Houston as soon as the house sells, but the houses aren't selling in our town. And that is why I am looking for employment. I need to help my mother pay the bills. Mother received divorce papers yesterday from his lawyer, but she cannot afford a lawyer to respond to his demands. Oh, I am sorry that I told you all that. Forgive me, please. I am so sorry."

Mrs. Samuelson said, "That is all right. I needed to know. Now let's talk about which days you can help me. Tell me your schedule, and we will put together a plan that will work for both of us."

Over the next hour they discussed what would work and which days wouldn't. Finally, the negotiations were finalized. Charlene would work two hours on Monday, Wednesday, and Friday and some hours Saturdays and Sundays if Mrs. Samuelson was planning a special event in her home. Mrs. Samuelson explained what she wanted done and how. Charlene carefully wrote down all instructions. On

Mondays, she would clean the second floor and bathrooms. On Wednesdays and Fridays, her attention would be directed to all rooms on the lower level. She promised Mrs. Samuelson she would do the best job she possibly could. She thanked her for having faith in her and giving her a chance. They agreed on a price per hour. Charlene thanked her for the Coke and conversation, and for the job. Then she said she needed to get home to help her mother. Also, she needed to do her homework.

Mrs. Samuelson walked her to the door, and as they said their goodbyes, Charlene said, "I'll see you Monday after school."

Charlene went home with a smile on her face. She had her first job. It wouldn't pay a lot of money, but it was a start. Now she could buy gym shoes and other school supplies, taking some pressure off her mother's limited paycheck.

She arrived home just as her mother was pulling into the driveway. She could hardly wait to tell her mother about having a job.

Her mother cried and said, "I am so proud of you." Through her sobs, she said, "I never dreamed that you would need to work to buy school supplies. Thank you for helping me. We will make it."

After dinner, Charlene did her homework and then wrote James a letter. There was so much to tell him.

Dear James,

Thank you for your letter about wintertime in Idaho. That sure doesn't sound like Wilsonville.

Pastor Jones helped me get a job. I will be working for Mrs. Samuelson. She lives in a gorgeous, old Victorian home that has a wide porch with a lot of gingerbread trim. I didn't know houses like that existed in Wilsonville. I will work two hours for her on Mondays, Wednesdays, and Fridays, and some on Saturdays and Sundays if she is holding a special event. She is such a sweet older lady, so gentle and kind. I want to do a good job for her. I want her to be happy.

She has taken a chance on hiring me. She encouraged me to keep up with my schoolwork. She wanted to know about my grades, what subjects I liked. She also wanted to know about my goals in the future. I told her I want to go to college. She was very encouraging.

The divorce papers came yesterday. Mother is just paralyzed not knowing what to do next. Life is so hard. I can't believe that it's already February. The time has stood still and has flown by all at the same time.

I still look at the Big Dipper on clear nights and think about you. I still miss you. Tell me more about the horse ranch and Idaho.

Your friend always,
Charlene

The weekend was filled with chores at home. She and her mother worked side by side doing laundry and cleaning house. They visited, and Charlene even got her mother to smile and giggle once. That made her feel good. Then Sunday was church day. Charlene always looked forward to hearing the choir sing and Pastor Jones preach his stirring messages.

Monday arrived. Charlene was happy to be going to school and seeing her friends. They all hung out together, talking about hopes and dreams for the future. Some of the girls were dating and of course talked about their boyfriends.

Soon the school day was over. Charlene dashed over to Mrs. Samuelson's home to begin her first day of work. She had a copy of the things Mrs. Samuelson wanted done, written on a three-by-five card. She kept it in her pocket. This way she could check off each job as it was completed.

But first Mrs. Samuelson wanted her to sit, have a Coke, and tell her about her day. They visited for a few minutes, and then Charlene said, "I really must get started on my work before my boss comes in and catches me sitting here and enjoying myself!"

Mrs. Samuelson laughed heartily. "Let me show you where I keep all the cleaning supplies."

And so, the first day of the new job began. Charlene preformed each task to perfection. The house was sparkling when she finished. She worked quickly and thoroughly.

She asked, "May I cut some of the flowers in your yard for a bouquet to place on the kitchen table?"

Mrs. Samuelson was very pleased with that suggestion.

When Charlene arrived home, her mother was already there.

Her mother said, "I had the most interesting thing happen today. A man in a business suit, carrying a briefcase, came in to where I work. He was asking for me. He is Jerimiah Schommley, attorney-at-law from one of the leading law firms in town. He said his firm had received word that I need a lawyer about a divorce issue. I said, 'Yes, I need a lawyer, but I cannot afford to pay you or any other lawyer.'

"He said, 'I understand. However, that is not a problem. An anonymous benefactor has hired our firm to take care of your divorce issue. It will not cost you anything.' My head dropped into my hands, and I began to cry.

"He assured me things will be taken care of and for me not to worry because they will take care of all the details. He just needs the divorce papers that were delivered to the house. He wanted to know the name of the company your dad works for, your dad's address, and how many months he hasn't sent us money. I am to deliver the papers to his office tomorrow. He said divorces across state lines are a little more time consuming and a little more difficult, but he will take care of the details. Oh, Charlene, there are good people in this world who are willing to help us. I am so thankful for whoever this angel of mercy is. May God bless him or her."

That night Margaret made a tuna salad for dinner. The pantry was almost bare. Only a half jar of peanut butter, a few slices of bread, and one can of tuna remained. Charlene wrote her daddy a letter.

Dear Daddy,

I am not sure how to begin this letter. Part of me still loves you, and part of me is very angry with you for what you have done to our family. And I guess it is the angry part of me that is writing this letter. While you are living high with your new love, I want you to know what life is like for your family. I have taken a job cleaning a house to have money to buy school supplies. Want to know what is in our pantry? One can of tuna, a half jar of peanut butter, and a few slices of bread. I hope you enjoy your lavish dinner with your new love tonight. When you look into your lovely dinner plate, I hope you will see a meager serving of tuna salad.

Your daughter,
Charlene

The next day Margaret delivered the divorce papers to the lawyer's office along with the other information Attorney Schommley had requested. And so, the process began.

The day following, Charlene dropped by the church to thank the pastor for directing her to Mrs. Samuelson. Then she asked him about the food pantry. Who is eligible to pick up food?

He quickly responded, "Anyone who has a need is eligible for food. Would you like one of our volunteers to drop a box by your house?"

She nodded and burst into tears. Through her sobs, she said, "We have one can of tuna, a few slices of bread, and a half jar of peanut butter. And that is all."

He reached over, patted her shoulder, and kindly said, "One of our men will deliver a box of food to your house. We will deliver a box to your house every week until you say there is no further need. You did right by coming to talk with me. It is going to be all right. Things will get better."

Charlene thanked him profusely. She left his office and went to the hospital to read to Peter. That little boy always made her feel better about things when she could visit with him. And he looked forward to her visits, too. After reading with him, she hurried home to be there when her mother arrived from work. Slowly their lives had worked out a routine, or was it a new normal?

When she arrived home, a large box of food sat beside the front door. She felt like it was Christmas.

She promised herself, "One day, if the good Lord allows it to happen, I want to be able to help hurting people." With a grateful heart, she carried the heavy box into the kitchen. She set it on the counter just as her mother entered the front door. Her mother saw the box and knew immediately where it had come from.

She said, "When your daddy was here, before the plant closed, we used to donate to the food pantry. Never in my wildest nightmares did I ever think one day I would be needing their help. Tonight, when we say grace over our meal, we must give God an extra thank-you for the food we will be eating."

When Charlene went to work at Mrs. Samuelson's home, she learned she would be needed over the weekend. Mrs. Samuelson would be hosting a tea for a club in which she was a member.

Charlene asked, "Exactly what all do you want me to help with? Please explain to me in detail your expectations. I have never been to a tea, so please educate me."

Mrs. Samuelson wanted her sterling silver tea service polished as well as her serving trays. On the day of the tea, Charlene would keep the refreshment trays filled with delicate sandwiches and sweets. She would need to refill the teapots, coffeepot, and punch bowl.

Mrs. Samuelson laid out a delicate, beautiful, little white apron for Charlene to wear. She would assist guests with their needs and just mingle with the group, getting to know them and them to know her.

After the tea was over and everything was cleaned up and items restored to their normal places, Charlene went home. She was tired but very happy that she'd had a chance to experience such a beautiful social event.

She dashed a note off to James.

Dear James,

 You would never guess what I had a chance to do for Mrs. Samuelson. She held a high tea at her house. She used silver serving pieces and the works. The table was amazing to see with its lace tablecloth with the gleaming silver trays loaded with beautiful, tiny sandwiches and pastries arranged on each. The ladies arrived wearing fancy hats and nice dresses. They all looked so lovely. I was working, but I must say I really enjoyed the social event from my point of view. I just had to tell you about it.

Your friend always,
Charlene

One week turned into another, and months rolled by. School was over for this year. Charlene was invited to attend a summer science camp. She received a scholarship so she could attend. She made arrangements with Mrs. Samuelson to be away for three weeks. Mrs. Samuelson was her biggest cheerleader.

 After work, when Charlene was leaving, Mrs. Samuelson gave her an envelope to be opened after she had left on her trip to camp. She had written Charlene a note of encouragement and enclosed three crisp, ten-dollar bills for spending money. Charlene felt her eyes begin to tear up. What an incredible lady! She would write her a thank-you note from camp and give her a report of expectations and activities.

 The three weeks flew by. During that time, she met students from other towns and cities. A whole new world was opening before her eyes. She could see she needed to take all the math and science classes Wilsonville High School had to offer.

 She snatched a few minutes of time to write Mrs. Samuelson and James. She sent a thank-you note to Mrs. Samuelson and told her what an amazing opportunity this was. She was beginning to see her future taking more shape and direction and wanted to thank Mrs. Samuelson for her encouragement and help.

When she wrote to James, she said,

Dear James,

You will never guess where I am. I have been selected to attend a three-week-long science camp. This camp is incredible. I can see that I need to take all the science and math classes Wilsonville High School has to offer. I wish you were here. You would dig right into the subject matter. You were always good at math and science. This note must be short. I need to get back to class. More later.

Your friend always,
Charlene

Charlene thought, *Tomorrow I must write Mother a note during my break time. I wish I could talk with her. I wish I knew how the divorce proceedings were going. But long-distance phone calls are just too expensive.*

Soon the three weeks were over, and Charlene returned to Wilsonville. There was so much to tell about her new experience. It seemed like a light had turned on in her mind as she dreamed of the future.

A letter from James was waiting for her. Hurriedly she opened it.

Dear Charlene,

Life on the ranch is wonderful. I wish you could be here and see the horses. Baby colts have been born and are so fun to watch. When they are first born, their legs are so long and wobbly that they can hardly stand up. When they can finally stand up, they try to reach down, and their noses can't touch the ground because their legs are so long. They are fun to watch. It takes some time for them to learn to stand and walk around. Then in no time they are racing with other baby colts.

I am learning to ride broncos. I plan to try my hand at bronco riding at rodeos. So far, the horses have bucked me off every time. Dad and the ranch foreman have a good time laughing at me when I go flying off a horse and land in the dirt. There are times I think the horse laughs too.

I am going to a school dance this weekend. I'll let you know how that turns out. Glad to hear about you being selected to attend a science camp. Was it held at one of the universities?

I am sorry to hear about your parents divorcing and the hard times for everyone in Wilsonville.

I still think of you when I see the Big Dipper on a clear night. Write soon.

Your friend always,
James

Margaret arrived home, thrilled to have Charlene waiting for her. They talked until late into the night, catching up on things that had happened in the past three weeks.

Attorney Jerimiah Schommley was working hard at resolving the divorce issue. He was working with an attorney in Houston. He hoped to have details worked out very soon.

Charlene's dad was very surprised when Margaret's lawyer contacted him. He was very angry. He called Margaret, and the conversation wasn't pleasant. He wanted the divorce to happen quickly. He wanted to know what she was doing, delaying things with all this legal stuff. And he also mentioned that he had received an angry letter from Charlene.

The summer came to an end. Cool fall temperatures turned into the cold winter months and were now turning back to springtime. Charlene's sophomore year was drawing to a close. Her daddy's salary had been garnished, and she and her mother were receiving a check each month for Charlene's support, plus money for the months when he had sent nothing. The checks would continue to be received until Charlene was out of school.

Her daddy was angry about that. He said the payments made life hard on him. After all, he had a new life and didn't want to be encumbered with a smaller paycheck each month. The divorce would be final in a couple of months. All details between the attorneys had been hammered out, and the attorney had seen to it that her daddy was sending money to support Charlene.

She explained to the pastor that her daddy was once again sending money. She thanked Pastor Jones and said, "I will repay every can and every pound of food as soon as I can get a good job. I will not forget. Thank you for helping us."

Pastor Jones replied, "That is why the food pantry is here. It is to help people during their time of need."

Charlene's junior year of school began. She continued to work for Mrs. Samuelson. Mrs. Samuelson had been such a large part of their lives that she felt like family. She encouraged Charlene to start applying at colleges and universities.

A new business moved into town. It was a Ben Franklin store. That would provide a few jobs. And maybe a few houses would sell as other new businesses began to come back. Outside of town, along the river in the deep valley, a large dam was to be built. That would bring opportunities for jobs. Plus, in the future, hotels and chain stores would move into town. Some were saying the area would eventually become a recreational area. Hope was beginning to grow in Wilsonville.

There was a guy in science lab; whose name was Sean, and he was always very friendly. He and Charlene had started kindergarten together. She liked him; she had never overtly encouraged his friendship, but she didn't discourage him either. He always seemed to be seated near her, or his station was next to hers in science lab. They laughed and joked but mostly challenged each other. Charlene competed with him much the same way she had with James. It was always a friendly rivalry.

On more than one occasion, he mentioned that the prom was approaching. One day he casually asked, "Do you have a date for the prom?"

Charlene stopped what she was doing and just stared at him. Rather startled, she said, "Why, no, I don't. I hadn't even thought about attending the prom."

He burst into laughter and said, "Well, get to thinking about it. I am asking you to go to the prom with me."

Margaret had received a promotion at work. And Attorney Schommley seemed to be calling Margaret more frequently. Charlene began to wonder whether he was interested in more than the divorce. Lately Margaret appeared to have a different outlook on life. She seemed to be more fun to be around. She laughed often.

Charlene thought, *have we finally made an upward turn? Life is getting better for us.*

Little Peter continued to be in and out of the hospital. Charlene visited him often. The health challenges of this little boy had stirred a deep interest in helping children. And just look at him. Now he was reading to her. He mostly just wanted to talk and hear about things at high school.

Letters from James continued.

Dear Charlene,

I am improving with bronc riding, though some of the landing are hard. I often have a mouth full of dirt from landing face first on the ground from being bucked off. Plus, I have been trying my hand at calf-roping contests. I have placed in some of the events. I am enjoying life on the ranch. I didn't know this lifestyle even existed until we moved here. High school is good. Yes, I am making good grades.

Do you remember that we promised to meet again on July Fourth at City Park when we are twenty-one? When you get your school pictures made, be sure to send me one. I would like to know what the little next-door-neighbor girl looks like. I will send you a picture, too.

Oh, back to us meeting in a few years. I have wondered what that meeting will be like. You are strong into academics, and I am not doing badly myself but nothing like you are. My rodeo schedule keeps me busy. I have dated some of the girls at school. Did I tell you that I do enjoy country western music and dancing? Life in Idaho has been good for my parents and for me.

I am sorry life has been so rough for you. Good luck with applying for admission at all those colleges and universities. I guess I better start doing that myself. I don't want you to get ahead of me. Write again soon.

Your friend always,
James

Charlene wrote back.

Dear James,

Your life sounds exciting and interesting. I cannot imagine what it is like to ride a horse, let alone be thrown from one. I prefer not having a mouth full of dirt. Ha-ha! The baby colts sound very cute. I would love to see them. Your life sounds free and open. My life is a set routine: school, work, school, work. You said you have been dating. I have a date for the prom. Now my next challenge is getting a dress for that night. I've never been to anything like that. Truth be known, I've never been on a date. My life has been rather plain. I don't know how to dance. Maybe Sean Stevenson can teach me. I suppose I should mention to him that I don't know how to dance. He is my partner in science lab. No dancing going on there. My mother is doing much better. It seems she has broken out into the sunshine at last. The past two years have been very hard on her.

Write again soon and tell me about life in Idaho. Yes, I will send you a picture. I am curious to see what the boy next door looks like in a cowboy hat. I'll try to send you a prom picture. Sean was in our classes when you were here. You will recognize him.

Your friend always,
Charlene

Within a few short days, Charlene received a letter from James.

Dear Charlene,

I wish I was there. I would teach you to dance. I think I do remember Sean. When you send me a prom picture, I will have a better idea.

I thought I should tell you that I broke my collarbone at the last rodeo. The bronco won that round. While I am out recuperating, I plan to really buckle down on my science and math classes. I can't let any little, ol' next-door-neighbor girl get ahead of me.

Write soon.

Your friend always,
James

The divorce was final. Margaret was sad but glad to get the long-drawn-out issue behind her. There should be no further interaction with George. His monthly check was to be deposited directly into the bank.

Time went by the way it does, and several weeks later, when Charlene came home from school, a car was parked at James's old home. Then another car pulled into the driveway. She was curious to see what was going on. A real estate agent got out of the first car and welcomed an older couple. They were discussing the house and size of the lot. Charlene was happy that some good person had mowed the lawn, and the place looked nice for a prospective buyer. They went into the house. But curiosity was just about to kill Charlene.

Soon her mother pulled into the driveway. She also saw the two vehicles in the driveway. She came into the house and asked Charlene, "What is going on next door?"

Charlene answered, "A real estate agent and an older couple are over there, looking at the property. I am about to explode with curiosity!"

They heard voices out in the yard. Under the pretext of getting something from the car, Margaret walked outside.

The real estate agent saw her and came across to introduce himself and his clients, Mr. and Mrs. Johannsson. The couple had lived in Wilsonville many, many years ago and decided to move back and make this their retirement home. They had looked at the property twice before, only during the daytime. This evening they had decided to purchase this home. Margaret and Charlene welcomed them to the neighborhood.

With excitement, Margaret and Charlene reentered their home. The winds of change were coming back to Wilsonville. Hope continued to grow in the neighborhood.

The phone was ringing when they walked into the house. It was Attorney Schommley. Margaret blushed as she took the phone from Charlene's hand.

Charlene smiled, winked at her, and left the room. She went to her room to work on homework and to write James.

Dear James,

There is so much to tell you that I am not sure where to begin. Someone is buying your family home, but I am sure you already know about that. They are an older couple and seem nice. I don't think I told you that a Ben Franklin store is coming to town. And the biggest news of all is that a dam is being built somewhere down across the river in the valley. I am not sure where it is being built. City planners are saying that since the lake will be backing up close to town, our town will someday be a resort area with boating and water sports businesses, hotel chains, and nice restaurants. Hope is returning to Wilsonville. At last we have something to get excited about.

Now to you. What is this? A broken collarbone? Better that than your neck. I think I like hearing that you have eaten dirt better than hearing that you have a broken bone.

I plan to talk with my guidance counselor this week about when to take the SAT and ACT tests. Have you checked on that? Have you applied to any colleges and universities? If so, where?

How was your school dance?

I will write again soon.

Your friend always,
Charlene

Charlene asked her mother whether it would be possible for her to buy a prom dress and shoes.

Margaret replied quickly, "Yes, Charlene, you have had to do without many things you have wanted these almost three years, and I would like you to buy the perfect one. It will be good to buy something someplace other than a second-hand store. We will get your hair fixed for the occasion. You will be lovely. Didn't you say you have a date for the prom?"

Charlene replied, "Yes, I am going with Sean. Some of the girls say that they color-coordinate with their dates. I haven't talked with Sean about colors yet. I think I'll do that tomorrow. I wish James was here."

Margaret laughed and then replied, "You two were inseparable when you were children. You fought like brother and sister. You did everything together. That old tree house was your special hideout. You two competed in everything."

Margaret's voice became wistful, and she said, "I miss those days."

The next day Charlene asked Sean about what color he preferred for the prom. He looked surprised. He replied, "I don't know. I just supposed the girls made those decisions. I do suggest you wear something in blue. You have a blue sweater that you *really* look good in. That sweater matches your eyes. I could get a blue cummerbund and bow tie to wear with my suit. When you get your dress, then I will match your colors."

Charlene said, "There is one more thing I need to tell you."

Sean looked rather puzzled and said, "Tell me what?"

She shyly said, "I don't know how to dance."

He laughed out loud, thus startling other students, who all looked at the two of them. He said, "I thought something was really wrong. That is no problem. I can teach you. Anyway, I will have the most beautiful date on the floor, so who cares if you can dance or not … with those baby-blue eyes and that blond hair? You will knock them dead. Man! Has anyone ever told you that you are beautiful? I am one lucky guy to have you as my date."

Charlene ducked her head and blushed, responding, "But Sean, I've never even been on a date. All I do is go to church, work, and school. I've never had time for that luxury."

He looked surprised and said, "Really? You are always surrounded by girls and guys."

She said, "I know. I just have a lot of sweet, understanding friends."

The teacher was coming their direction. Charlene said, "Quick, get busy. We have a supervisor about to arrive. We need to complete this experiment."

After school Sean met Charlene and asked whether she would like a ride home.

She replied, "Actually, I am on the way to the hospital to visit a little boy I have been visiting with for well over two years. He has an incurable disease, and I always visit him when he is hospitalized. Sean, I am beginning to think I may go into the medical field on some level."

Sean responded, "That is okay. I will drop you off at the hospital. And, I am not surprised that you may enter the medical field. You have a certain tenderness and compassion I do not see in many of our friends. Here is my truck. Hop in." He had an old, beat-up Ford pickup that had many miles on it; all the dents, scrapes and fading paint gave it a certain touch of character.

Charlene smiled when she saw it. She liked it. This wasn't a pretentious, high-dollar, chick-magnet automobile.

She asked him what he planned to do with his life. He was silent for a few minutes, then replied, "I am thinking of something similar to your choice, only I am interested in genetics."

She asked, "Any particular reason you are thinking of genetics?"

He reflected, and after a great deal of thought, he replied, "Yes, males in my family tend to die early of heart attacks. Our family doctor said it is inherited."

Quickly changing the subject, he asked whether she had mailed letters of inquiry to colleges and universities, and if so, which ones? He wanted to know whether she was in the running for any scholarships, and so went the conversation by two highly motivated young people.

Sean stopped at the hospital, and Charlene got out. She thanked him for the ride and said, "I'll see you in class tomorrow." With a wave, she dashed into the hospital.

Little Peter was heavily medicated, and numerous tubes and machines were attached to him. His mother and father, Ruth and Charles Smith, were seated beside him. In shock, Charlene gasped when she saw Peter was attached to so many machines. She had never met Peter's parents before. Gaining her composure, she introduced herself and said she was the student who had been reading with Peter for the past two years. The couple stood to their feet and shook her hand, saying how much Peter loved her and appreciated all the visits. They conveyed how much they appreciated her encouragement to a very sick little boy.

Peter's dad, Charles, said, "Peter has a very rare form of cancer. We have taken him to Mayo Clinic and various children's cancer research centers, attempting to get help for our son."

Peter's mother, Ruth, continued, "The doctor says Peter may not make it to this weekend." And she began sobbing softly. Her husband wrapped his arms around her, holding her tightly, with tears streaming down his own face.

Charlene said, "I am so sorry. I didn't know what he was suffering from. He didn't put a name to it. He just said he has a rare disease. Is there anything I can do for you? Do you know Pastor Jones? Why, yes, I am sure you do, because he suggested that I read with Peter, beginning some two years ago. Can I call him for you?"

Charles replied, "Thank you. He just left a few minutes ago. He said he will stop by again a little later."

About that time, Dr. Hayden came in. He said, "Hello, Charlene. Glad to see you again. I guess Charles and Ruth have told you our boy is not doing well."

Charlene nodded. She didn't trust her voice. She could feel her emotions rising.

Then he said, "Charlene, I think I need to spend some time with Ruth and Charles. Will you please excuse us? Oh wait. Before you go, can I call you sometime? I have something I would like to talk about with you."

As she was leaving, she shook hands with Charles and hugged Ruth, who clung to her, weeping with body-wracking sobs.

Charlene said, "Dr. Hayden, I will await your phone call." She reached over and tenderly touched little Peter's arm. Then she slipped out the door, closing it quietly behind her.

When she exited the hospital doors, she leaned her head against a huge column and began to sob. A hand touched her shoulder, and she looked up to see Sean standing beside her. She turned to him, and he engulfed her in his arms, holding her as she cried over little Peter's hopeless condition.

Through her sobs, she said, "Sean, Peter is dying. I know what I want to do in life. I want to go into cancer research. I want to fight and kill this beast. If God will help me, I will fight this horrible disease!" And a second wave of sobs engulfed her.

Sean held her tightly until she had begun to regain control, then softly said, "Come on. Let's go get a Coke."

Charlene said, "I can't. I don't have any money on me."

He jokingly said, "Silly, I invited you to go with *me* for a Coke! It is my treat."

She looked at him through red, tear-filled eyes and smiled. "Thank you. I am so used to doing for myself. I didn't think of that. Thank you."

They started walking toward the pickup. She stopped and turned to face him and said, "Hey! Wait a second. How did you know I would be coming out so soon?"

Sean said, "Little Peter is my next-door neighbor. We had heard that he doesn't have much time left. When you first started reading with Peter, his mother asked me if I knew who you were. I said, 'Yes, she is in my classes, and I said some more stuff.' Anyway, I knew you would be coming out, so I waited for you. I wanted to tell you but just didn't know how. Knowing when and how to say things isn't like putting a formula into a test tube. I am sorry. I hope I didn't do something wrong."

Charlene said, "No, you did nothing wrong. I understand. But I admit that I was really shocked when I saw all those tubes and machines attached to that little person."

They resumed their walk to the pickup. She stopped once more, looked up at him, and said, "Thank you for waiting for me. That was sweet. I needed you right then."

Saying nothing, he reached over and squeezed her hand.

The two friends discussed many things. Sean asked about her family. She shared with him all that had happened in over two years since her daddy had left home to find work. She told him about working for Mrs. Samuelson and said what a beautiful person she was.

He told his own story about the struggles the family had experienced after the plant closed to move overseas. His dad worked out of town and came home weekends. Sean had a paper route, and he made deliveries and did odd jobs for the drugstore, plus mowing the grass for neighbors. Anything to earn a little money to help his parents.

They agreed that just about everyone in Wilsonville has had his or her struggles. Both agreed that they must hold onto their hopes and dreams because this hard place in life isn't forever.

Sean was dropping her off at her home just as Margaret pulled into the driveway. Margaret walked over to the old, beat-up pickup to meet Sean.

She said, "So you are the Sean my daughter has been talking about. I don't think I have seen you since you and Charlene were in elementary school. I understand you are one smart kid. Charlene likes that. She likes to be challenged by your success in math and science. And, oh yes, there is a prom coming up, I understand." She smiled and said, "Please tell your parents hello. It is nice seeing you again. It is always good to see Charlene's friends." With that she walked into the house.

Charlene told Sean goodbye and said, "I'll see you tomorrow. Thank you for the Coke and most of all for being there for me this afternoon. I really, really appreciate it."

She walked to the house and turned to wave at Sean. He waited until she was on the front porch before driving away.

School pictures came in. Charlene and Sean exchanged pictures.

Margaret had begun preparing the evening meal when Charlene entered the kitchen. She told her mother about Sean taking her to the hospital to see little Peter. She shared about Peter's grave condition, about Dr. Hayden wanting to talk with her sometime, and about

Sean having waited for her. She left out no details, including the part about wanting to go into cancer research.

Her mother listened to all Charlene had to say. Then she said, "I am sorry about little Peter. That is sad. But that is wonderful that Dr. Hayden wants to talk. I am so very proud of you."

There was a short period of silence when Margaret said, "I have some news for you, too. Attorney Schommley called and asked me to go to dinner with him this Friday night."

Charlene said, "That is exciting! Where is he taking you?"

Margaret said, "I am not sure. He said he knows of a good restaurant in a neighboring town. Now I need to go shopping to get a new dress. It has been a long time since I bought something new. I've bought our clothes from secondhand stores for so long that I almost don't remember what it is like to go into a real store. And speaking of new dresses, this Saturday, if Mrs. Samuelson doesn't need you to work, why don't we go look for a prom dress?"

And so plans were set in motion for a shopping trip.

After dinner Charlene went to her room to work on trigonometry. She had completed algebra and geometry; next would be calculus. Her guidance counselor was helping her enroll in as many math and science classes as she could schedule in high school. The counselor was positive she would have to take a course or two from a neighboring college, perhaps even as a night courses, if need be. The counselor was checking on that. Charlene knew she may need to take a summer course or two in a neighboring town to have all the science and math blocks checked off her educational plan. She hoped that wouldn't be the case. It would be hard to get transportation to the college.

At least it was the counselor's plan to send her to the junior college to pick up any courses not offered at Wilsonville High School. Her senior year would be no walk in the park. She would have to work very hard to maintain her grade point average in higher mathematical courses as well as the science classes. She had told her counselor about her plans to go into research. The counselor had to do some research of her own to help Charlene with her educational tract. She had only one other student who was as driven and determined to achieve a goal. It was an amazing thing to see. Many students seemed to sluff off during the last year of school. Not Charlene. And yet Charlene had maintained an A average in all the upper-level courses.

Unknown to Charlene, the counselor had contacted the local hospital to discuss how best to prepare a gifted student for a degree in the medical field of research. She was given in-depth instructions as to what was required. The counselor asked whether there was any chance that Charlene might receive a scholarship to a university.

Inquiries were sent to various universities on the behalf of Charlene and one other student. The counselor explained some of the difficulties and painful experiences her student had encountered; yet despite all her challenges, she never lost sight of her goal. Even in the most difficult of times, Charlene had managed to keep her goal in sight. If an impoverished student could achieve what she had endured, then there was no excuse for students who had a rough time saying they couldn't get an education.

Charlene proved that if you want something bad enough, you will do it.

She took a break from her studies to write James a letter and try to clear her head before resuming trig homework.

Dear James,

I have so much to tell you. First, before I start telling you everything, here is one of my school pictures. On the back, I have written a message to you. It says, "Here is a picture of the girl next door. Don't forget to meet me at the gazebo on July Fourth when we turn twenty-one years of age. Charlene."

Let me start today's letter off with science lab. Sean and I were talking about the prom during the time we were working on a lab experiment. I asked him what color he would like for us to coordinate for the prom. He paid me the sweetest compliment. He mentioned one of my blue sweaters he really likes. He said that I look good in it because the blue matches my eyes. He wants that color if I can find it in the right dress.

When I said that I don't know how to dance, he laughed and said he will teach me. Then he said, "Anyway, you will be the most beautiful girl on the floor, so no one will notice if you are dancing or not. They will just be looking at your long, blond hair and those blue eyes. I will be the luckiest guy on the floor to have you for my date." Wasn't that a sweet thing to say? Also, he gave me a ride in his pickup to the hospital to visit little Peter, who has been hospitalized again.

When I went in to see Peter, his parents were there, and Peter was attached to all sorts of tubes and machines. His parents said he may not make it to the weekend.

When I left to go home, I held it together until I was out of the building. I made it to those big columns at the entrance to the hospital and I began to cry. I didn't know anyone was around until I felt a hand on my shoulder. It was Sean. Peter is Sean's next-door neighbor.

Sean knew how bad Peter was and knew I wouldn't be inside very long, so he waited for me. I didn't know he was waiting. He held me in his arms while I cried like crazy in front of the hospital—in public!

That is when it hit me what I want to study in college. I want to go into cancer research. I told Sean that is what I want to do. I want to fight cancer. I will become a doctor. After seeing what it has done to sweet, little Peter, I want to defeat this beast. Every time I see a cancer cell under a microscope, I will think of little Peter.

I better get back to work on my trig.

Write again soon.

Your friend always,
Charlene

The next day after school, Sean gave Charlene a ride to Mrs. Samuelson's home.

When Charlene approached the door, Mrs. Samuelson met her. She said, "Well, look at you. And who might the young man be?"

Charlene told her all about Sean and said he was her partner in science lab. He was taking all the same upper-level math and science classes she was. She said he had asked her to the prom. She continued, "But Mrs. Samuelson, I don't know how to dance! I've never even been on a date. I don't have time for dating. I am trying to maintain my grade point average. I am hoping to earn a scholarship.

"Oh, Mrs. Samuelson, the little boy I read to each week is in the hospital and is dying of cancer. I am just heartbroken over that fact. Because of him, I plan to become a cancer research scientist. I want to kill this beastly disease."

And once more tears splashed down her cheeks. Mrs. Samuelson took her in her arms and just held her.

She said, "You will be a success at whatever you do. Now, we need to teach you how to dance. When is this prom? How much time do we have? Does Sean dance? I know his parents. He comes from a good family."

Charlene responded, "Yes, he dances, and he said that he can teach me. But we have no time. He works a couple of jobs and is carrying a heavy class load too, just as I am. He is really a good guy."

Mrs. Samuelson disappeared into another room, and Charlene went to the second floor to begin her chores. She was working as hard, as thoroughly, and as fast as she could. She wanted to please Mrs. Samuelson.

The motor of the vacuum cleaner suddenly stopped. Mrs. Samuelson was standing in the doorway. She had unplugged the vacuum cleaner. She said, "Charlene, can you come downstairs for a moment?"

Curious, Charlene followed her down to the first floor. There stood Sean!

Smiling, Charlene said, "Sean, what are you doing here?"

He and Mrs. Samuelson were both smiling. Sean said, "I understand that a dance instructor is needed this afternoon." All three joined in a hearty laugh. By now Mrs. Samuelson had music going, and Sean reached out a hand to Charlene, and so dance lesson number one began.

An hour sped by in no time. It would have been difficult for a bystander to say who had the most fun, Charlene and Sean or Mrs. Samuelson.

Charlene thanked Sean and Mrs. Samuelson for a most enjoyable hour. Then she asked, "Mrs. Samuelson, if it is all right with you, I will come back tomorrow afternoon and finished my Monday's work."

Mrs. Samuelson responded, "Why, Charlene, if that is what you would like to do, that is fine with me."

Sean was happy to give Charlene a ride to her home. They laughed and teased each other all the way across town about some of Charlene's newly invented dance steps. Soon the old pickup pulled in the driveway. Charlene thanked him for his patience with her dancing and for the ride home. She waved at him as he drove away.

When Charlene entered the house, the phone was ringing. The voice on the other end of the line said, "This is Pastor Jones. I thought you might want to know that little Peter passed away this morning. We will let you know when the funeral is to be held. Mr. and Mrs. Smith asked that I notify you."

A stunned Charlene said, "Thank you, Pastor Jones, for letting me know." She hung up the phone and said, "Goodbye, little Peter."

Margaret came through the door shortly after Pastor Jones's phone call. Now Charlene had her mother to talk to about this little boy.

Then Margaret placed a stack of mail on the table. Most of it was junk mail, but toward the bottom was a letter from George. Margaret said, "What is this? Why am I hearing from him?" She ripped open the envelope and angrily yanked out the letter.

Dear Margaret and Charlene,

I have some news I want to share with you. I have broken up with my girlfriend. I am quitting my job and want to come home so we can be a family once again. Surely, I can get a job on the construction of the dam. Please let me know by return mail if I can come home.

I love and miss you both.

George

Margaret's eyes blazed, and her face flushed with anger. She said, "Not on your life! After all you have put us through, and now you want to come home? I think not! We had to get food from the food pantry just to live. Charlene had to get a job cleaning a house just to buy school supplies. And now suddenly you want to come home? Hmm, just because he broke up with his lady friend. No, thank you!"

She stormed around the kitchen, slamming pots and pans and rattling dishes.

Then she stopped and said, "I am writing him a letter right now, even before I make supper. I plan to take it to the post office immediately."

Charlene sat back and said nothing. She had never seen her mother so angry and hurt. All the pent-up anger, pain, and suffering from over three years had come boiling out.

Charlene thought, *It is a good thing he doesn't walk through the front door right now.*

Then the phone rang. Margaret grabbed the phone and loudly said, "*Hello.*"

The voice on the other end said, "Margaret? Is that you? This is Jerimiah."

A startled and embarrassed Margaret attempted to regain her composure. She said, "Yes, Jerimiah, it is me. You caught me at a very bad moment. My ex-husband has decided he wants to come home. I guess I overreacted and let my anger get away from me. Sorry if I broke your eardrum."

He chuckled and replied, "I am fine. I wanted to know whether you and Charlene would like to go out to dinner this evening. Nothing fancy. The Pizza Hut has some pretty good pizza if you two would like to join me."

Margaret was still trying to recover from her embarrassing, angry outburst and said, "Let me check with Charlene. Can you hold a second? Charlene, would you like to go to Pizza Hut with Jerimiah and me? I promise we will have you back in plenty of time to do your homework."

And so, Jerimiah rescued a doomed evening. He picked them up at seven o'clock.

He impressed Charlene, though she was skeptical at first.

He asked, "What grade are you in?"

She replied that she was a junior.

Next, he asked what subjects she liked.

She explained that math and science were her major focus. She wanted to become a cancer research scientist.

He said, "Whoa! Don't you have to take a lot of upper-level math and science classes to enter that field?"

She explained that she was working closely with her guidance counselor. To have all the courses she needed, she would need to pick up some classes at a junior college during the summer.

After listening to her, he said, "It sounds like you have a plan and definite goals in mind. Hold on to your dreams."

Then he turned his focus to Margaret. "How does this latest news from your ex fit into your plans for the future?"

She quickly responded, "He had his chances, and he blew it. There is no place in my future for him. End of subject. Now, tell Charlene about your good news."

He smiled and said, "I have been offered a full partnership in the firm."

Charlene said, "Congratulations. Since I have absolutely no knowledge of the hierarchy in a law firm, I am assuming this is a big deal. You must be feeling a great sense of pride and accomplishment."

He laughed heartily, agreeing that he was very pleased and honored to have this opportunity.

Margaret said, "It seems that Wilsonville is in a recovery stage. I still miss all of our friends who have moved to other places."

Jerimiah responded, "I am sure you do miss your old friends, but there are a lot of new people coming in to make friends with. They want to fit into the community and are hoping to form friendships too."

After they had eaten, Margaret and Jerimiah dropped Charlene off at the house so she could get started on her homework. They were going for a drive in the country.

Before beginning her homework, Charlene wrote to James.

Dear James,

What a crazy up-and-down day this has been. When you read my letters, you must think you are reading a soap opera.

Today was my day to work at Mrs. Samuelson's house. I had worked about an hour when she called me downstairs. There was Sean! She had called him to come over for a few minutes and to begin to teach me how to dance. I had told her I didn't know how, and she was seeing to it that I will be prepared on prom night. She laughed solidly for an hour. I guess I must have been pretty funny.

Then Sean gave me a ride home. After I was home, mother picked up the mail and came into the kitchen. She shuffled through the mail, throwing out the junk mail, when she came across a letter from Daddy, saying he broke up with his girlfriend and wanted to come home, like nothing ever happened. Mother threw one more hissy fit. She was still at the boiling point when the phone rang. It was Jerimiah, the attorney who took care of the divorce.

He and mother are dating. Not too sure what he thought by the way she answered the phone, but he hung in there and then invited us to go to Pizza Hut with him. We had a good evening. He is a very likable guy. I am not sure what I thought a lawyer would be like. Anyway, I like him.

Oh, one more thing. Little Peter died. I am terribly sad about that. I better get to work on homework. Oh, oh, one *more* thing. How is your collarbone?

Your friend always,
Charlene

Charlene had just finished her homework when the phone rang. It was Dr. Hayden.

He asked, "Is this a good time to talk?"

She answered, "Yes, I am just finishing my homework. Now is a fine time."

He said, "I like to have a high school student who is interested in the medical field to shadow some of the lab techs and learn the way around a hospital laboratory. Would you like to be that student? Large city hospitals do not do this as far as I know. But small-town hospitals tend to have a chance for the people touch. If you can spare an afternoon or two a week, I would love to introduce you to the head of the laboratory. From what I understand, you are interested in cancer research. This experience might give you a small introduction to what goes on with the blood that is drawn from patients down to tissue samples, et cetera. Are you interested?"

Charlene gasped. "I am indeed interested! I work two hours on Mondays, Wednesdays, and Fridays. I used to visit little Peter on Tuesdays and Thursdays each time he was in the hospital. When would you like for me to come by for an interview?"

Dr. Hayden said, "Drop by on your next free day, and someone will show you around."

Charlene thanked him profusely.

Reaching over, she picked up James's letter. Happily, she hadn't sealed it yet. She added a big PS.

James, the most amazing thing just happened! Dr. Hayden just called and invited me to shadow a lab tech at the hospital. He knows I want to go into cancer research, and he wants to introduce me to some of the things going on in the lab with body fluids, blood, tissue samples, etc. I am so excited I could pop! Bye again.

Saturday arrived. Charlene didn't have to work for Mrs. Samuelson, so she and her mother went shopping. It had been so long since they had been shopping together. They looked at dresses and shoes, walking from store to store, until they found the perfect dress. It was a blue, A-line, floor-length chiffon dress with lace appliqué, sequins, and beading on the bodice. When she saw herself in the mirror, she was surprised by the attractive young woman staring back at her. Then she thought, *Oh! That is me.*

Margaret searched until she found a pair of shoes that complemented the dress. She smiled at her daughter and said, "You are lovely!"

Charlene couldn't wait to see Sean and tell him about her dress. For many girls, a new prom dress may not be a big deal, but for her it was something extraordinary. The prom was one week away, and the last week of school was fast approaching.

Monday morning, while Charlene was in her first-period class, an office aide came into the classroom and said the guidance counselor needed to see her. Walking down the hallway, Charlene asked the girl what the guidance counselor wanted her for.

She said, "I don't know. She just said she needed to see you right away."

By now they were at the counseling office. Charlene walked in and was immediately invited into the counselor's office.

She asked Charlene to close the door. Then she said, "Charlene, I have some very good news. A group has agreed to scholarship you for summer school at the junior college. I have enrolled you in calculus and physics classes. Both are courses that we do not currently offer here at this high school. I think with the courses you are going to complete your senior year, you will be well prepared for college. Congratulations. A lot of people are pulling for you. You are well loved in this community. Again, congratulations."

Returning to her classroom, Charlene's head was spinning. How would she possibly keep her mind on her studies today after receiving this information? And after school on Tuesdays and Thursdays, she was to go to the hospital and shadow a lab tech, watching him or her work and listening to what he or she had to say. Her instructions were "Watch, listen, and learn." Excitement oozed from every pore of her body.

That afternoon she went to work for Mrs. Samuelson, who was delighted to hear all the good news. She told Mrs. Samuelson about her prom dress and shoes and said how happy she was to have them. She said, "Sean will have a blue cummerbund and bow tie."

Charlene sometimes wondered whether Mrs. Samuelson really needed the household help or whether she needed to hear all the happenings in her life. What a sweet lady she was. Such an encourager.

And yes, Sean appeared about ninety minutes into her work time to give her another quick dance lesson. When he arrived, he apologized because he couldn't come earlier. He had to make a delivery for the drugstore to an elderly couple out in the country, and it had taken longer than anticipated. The dance lesson went a smidgeon better than last time. Maybe she was catching on after all. Sean drove her home. He had another delivery to make for the drugstore.

Tuesday morning arrived with all the usual daily activities, and soon the day was over. Sean dropped her by the hospital for her new learning experience. She hoped the lab techs would allow her to look into the microscope. She didn't know what to expect. She had found microorganisms very fascinating when they were doing labs at school. She knew there were miniscule creatures she had never seen nor heard about, but she was eager to learn about them.

As she approached the lab, Dr. Hayden walked down the hall and joined her.

He said, "First, we need to get you into a lab coat, a *lovely cap,* mask, goggles, shoe coverings, and gloves. Okay, that is good. Now,

I have a few minutes, and I want to introduce you to the lab team. They are some of the best anywhere around."

Charlene thought, *I am fortunate that I have my hair up in a ponytail. That is the only way I could get all this hair under one of these blue caps.*

They were all friendly, kind, and gracious. They had been briefed on what she would be doing in the lab, much the same as students from other years. She and Dr. Hayden were walking past one station when a lab tech said, "Charlene, do you want to look at this? A surgeon has just finished surgery on a patient, and they want us to examine this sample of tissue. Let's see what is inside this tumor. If the patient is lucky, it will be nothing serious." He continued talking as he placed one slide after another slide of thin layers of tissue under the microscope.

He said, "I think this might need to be investigated more. I will pass this one off to the lab supervisor for a second opinion. Do you want to see healthy tissue? Look at this closely. Now, look at this slide. What do you see? That wasn't fair. Let me explain the differences. These are cancer cells, and this slide is healthy tissue. Look at them carefully. Look at the groupings of cells on the cancerous tissue.

"Next step is to determine which strain of cancer it is. If you like, in the weeks to come, when we have time, I will show you slides we have on file of various cancer cells." And so, the conversation went. The two hours she was in the lab flew by in no time. She had been allowed to see all sorts of things under a microscope, including amebic meningoencephalitis cells. She had seen other amoeba in lab at school but never this one.

She said, "There is a whole world of tiny creatures that we never see that are living on us and in us." The technician agreed.

Charlene was in awe at what she had seen. She couldn't wait for Thursday to arrive. She thanked the team, telling them she would see them on Thursday. She removed her protective coverings and was exiting the lab just as the lab supervisor caught up with her.

She said, "Charlene, please keep a log of the hours you are in the lab. Write down what type of cells you have seen, tissue samples, et cetera. Did anyone tell you that you are getting extra credit for working in the lab? It is imperative that you keep meticulous notes. I will be signing off on your logs. It is a joy to have you in the lab. Feel free to ask questions regarding anything you do not understand. I look forward to seeing you on Thursday."

On the way home, she stopped by a store and bought a thick spiral notebook to keep lab records in. Her first entry would be today. She would have the lab supervisor sign it on Thursday.

Fortunately, Wilsonville was a small town, so Charlene walked or rode her bicycle everywhere she went. Many people walked and rode bicycles to save on gasoline bills. Low-income family's do all they can to economize. As she walked home, she recounted her day. It was exciting to have these things to think about.

When she arrived home, Charlene saw a stack of suitcases and packages piled on the porch. She looked it over and was curious about what all that stuff was doing there. As she walked into the house, Margaret was already there, starting dinner and waiting for her. She handed Charlene a letter. It was from James.

Dear Charlene,

I hope things are going well for you. I have not started back to bronco riding. The doctor has not released me. There is something I must tell you. I am dating someone. She is really a nice girl, and I like her a lot. She heard me talking about you and got really mad at me. She wants me to stop writing to you. It hurts to tell you this because I enjoy your letters and like to hear of your progress in so many things. After all, we have known each other forever. I guess this will be my last letter to you. I am sorry.

I will always be your friend.

James

PS: I really like the picture of the little girl next door. Sean has good eyesight.

A stunned Charlene just stood in the kitchen floor, not knowing what to say or think. She had never thought this day would come. After all, there had always been James.

Finally, she found her voice. She told her mother about everything that had happened today. "Mother, you were right. We will get through these hard times and will be better for them. We will make it. There are so many good people who are willing to help when they see that someone is willing to work and try to better themselves and their community. If you don't mind, I think I will go write James a letter before I begin my homework."

Margaret said, "Charlene, there is something I need to tell you. I have had new locks put on the doors. I have a new key for you. When you have a chance, put your old key over here, and I will dispose of it."

Charlene said, "What has happened? Has someone been in our house? And what is that stuff on our porch?"

Margaret answered, "Your daddy came back today and put all of his stuff *in* the house while I was gone. The neighbors called me. I called Jerimiah, who called the police. By the time we all arrived at the house, he was gone. But all his stuff was in the living room. He has decided that he will stay here. *He* decided. He didn't ask. Jerimiah has helped me with the problem. The police told me I could pile his stuff on the porch and said to change the locks immediately. If or when he comes back, I'm supposed to call them. They will come out to make sure he leaves peacefully. George is not taking no for an answer. Anyway, we have had to change the locks.

"Oh, Charlene, I have missed the better part of a day of work. My paycheck will be smaller this month. I am so sorry.

"After him saying he never wanted to come back to Wilsonville again, why would he keep his house key all this time? He has no job. I'm sorry to say that your support money has stopped. We must tighten our belts once more. I am glad we could save some of the support money for a rainy day, because I think a storm cloud is brewing. Just about the time that I think we have made it into the sunshine, something else happens. But we will make it."

Slowly Charlene turned and walked out of the room. She went into her room and began a letter to James.

Dear James,

You said that you couldn't write to me anymore but didn't say I couldn't write to you. I hope you noticed what I had written on the back of my school picture. You don't have to write anything, but I still would like to have a picture of the boy next door wearing a cowboy hat. I have received a scholarship to attend summer school. I will be taking two college courses at a junior college in a nearby town.

Also, today I started shadowing a lab tech, or a bunch of them, at the hospital four hours a week. The supervisor of the lab said that my lab experience is for credit. I didn't know that in the beginning. I am to maintain a log of days and hours that I am in the lab.

My dance lessons are coming along. That is all I have to say about that. Not my most sterling moments.

Since I last wrote to you, we attended little Peter's funeral. I stood beside his little casket and promised him I will help researchers fight and beat cancer. I promised him.

Did I tell you that a Kmart has come into town? Slowly but slowly, Wilsonville is making a comeback.

Mother has had to have the locks changed on the doors. Daddy broke up with his girlfriend, quit his job in Texas, and is back in town. He thinks he is going to move in with us. Not going to happen!

Mrs. Samuelson is such a darling. I think she enjoys hearing about life at the high school more than she likes a sparkling-clean house. She gets so excited over the things

I tell her. Since my best friend is no longer in Wilsonville, I tell her all my secrets.

Your friend always,
Charlene

PS: Next week I will send you a copy of my prom picture.

PS #2: On a clear night, at eight o'clock, I still look at the Big Dipper and think of you.

After eating dinner and helping her mother clean up the kitchen, Charlene made entries in her lab log. She closed her eyes and started with the first lab tech who called her to his station to look at cancer cells; then she looked at the amoeba that causes meningitis. She named each cell and tissue sample she could remember.

Next was the homework routine, and finally her day came to an end. She was exhausted. Tomorrow she would be going to Mrs. Samuelson's home and perhaps have another dance lesson? *Poor Sean! He is really a good guy … such a good sport.*

Suddenly, there was loud banging on the front door. Someone was trying to get into the house.

Margaret looked outside and saw George. She told him, "Get your things and go away. You are not welcome here."

He yelled, "I want to come in and talk to you. Please let me in!"

Charlene was in her room, crying.

Margaret called Jerimiah, who called the police.

While George was still yelling and beating on the door, a car with flashing lights pulled into the driveway. Two policemen got out of the car.

George turned around and said, "This is *my* house. That is *my* family in there."

Jerimiah arrived and was now parked in the street. He got out of his car and stood behind the policemen. He said, "They *were* your family before you dumped them for another woman. You wanted a divorce so you could be with the other woman. In the divorce decree, you gave Margaret the house. You forfeited your rights to that house. I suggest you get your things and be on your way."

The policemen were walking toward the house.

George said, "Look, so I made a mistake. But man, oh man, she was a looker!" And he slapped his cap on his leg for emphasis. "Everyone makes a mistake one time or another. Anyway, I've changed my mind. Now I just want my family back. I love them."

One of the policemen said, "You have been gone for over three years. You have no idea what you have put Margaret and Charlene through. Don't you know that you can't come waltzing back in here like nothing ever happened? Anyway, you sure have a strange way of showing love. I suggest you remove your things from that porch and get going, or I am going to charge you with trespassing and harassment. Say, have you been drinking? If you like, you can sleep it off down in the county jail."

George said, "But officer, let me explain."

The policeman said, "I don't think there is anything left to explain. Do you want to have a restraining order slapped on you also?"

George picked up his bags and parcels and carried them back to his truck. He looked back at the house. Charlene looked out her bedroom window. She was crying, and Margaret was watching. She had the curtain pushed back from the window on the door. They both watched the police escort him to his truck. Soon the truck motor could be heard; then he drove down the street and out of sight.

The police and Jerimiah came into the house to talk with Margaret. The police said they would patrol the neighborhood frequently. They didn't expect any further trouble. They told her to call again if there was anything she felt uncomfortable about. And then they left. Jerimiah stayed with them for several hours.

The next day after school, Charlene went to visit Pastor Jones. She told him about her daddy suddenly coming back to town and the ruckus he had caused the night before.

Charlene said, "I am so embarrassed, angry, and hurt by him."

Pastor Jones said, "I know you and your mother have been hurt deeply, but before you or your mother can heal, you must forgive him. Forgiving him doesn't mean approving of his bad behavior. You are simply releasing the problem to God. He will take care of the problem. Then you can move on. True, what he has done is wrong and hurtful. But do not keep wounding yourselves by holding a grudge against him and even hating him in your hearts. By holding on to the pain and reliving the bad memories of what he has done, you can physically harm your own body."

Charlene asked, "How can we do this forgiveness thing? He has ripped our hearts out of our chests with his words and actions."

Pastor Jones replied, "It is not easy. It is hard, but it is easier than carrying around all the heavy baggage from being so deeply wounded. You need to pray to God and ask Him to help you find a way to forgive your dad for the pain and suffering he has brought on his family. You and God can work through this. Talk with God. He is waiting to hear from you."

Deep in thought, Charlene sat thinking about what the pastor had just said.

Then she said, "Okay, thank you, Pastor. I need to get going. I must stay on schedule."

Pastor Jones said, "Charlene, if you and your mother need a food box, please let me know."

She paused, shifted her weight, looked at the floor, hesitated some more, and then replied, "Mum, thank you. I will. In the meantime, give it to someone who needs it more than we do. Thank you, Pastor. I really appreciate it. One more thing. Pastor, why is life so hard? Mother and I are trying as hard as we know how to do right and to hold our heads up, yet it seems we take one step forward and then slide backward two steps. When will we break out of this? It feels like we are being punished for something we haven't done."

"Charlene," the pastor replied, "there are times in life when God allows us to be tested. Depending on how we handle the problem and what we learn about ourselves during that testing time, the trial is very valuable. God loves you and knows what you are going through.

So far, you have shown Him, me, and the community that you won't be defeated by things in life, by bad things you didn't create.

"You see, Charlene, people have been asking similar questions from the beginning of time. All I can say is, keep on trying and doing good. Keep fighting! Whatever you do, do not give up.

"You are making tremendous progress with your education. A lot of people are pulling for you. Look at the scholarship you have received for summer school. Look at the position you have as a student in the hospital lab. You have many things to be thankful for. Dwell on those things and not on the negative things that can cloud your vision. You are doing a good job. Keep on keeping on!

"You are approaching your senior year. Soon you will be going off to college and will be stepping out into your new life. Right now, is preparation time for you. Think of it this way. You are laying a foundation for your entire life that is ahead of you. That foundation is being built on a solid rock, not shifting sands. You have excellent grades, which should earn you a *pretty nice* scholarship. Hold on to your dreams, Charlene. Just hold on.

"Be sure to be in church on Sunday. I think my message may have some information you may want to hear.

"Oh yes. I understand the prom is this coming weekend. Please drop by after it is over and tell me about it. Okay? Now you need to get to your next appointment before you are late. I will be praying for you."

"Thank you, Pastor Jones. I appreciate you so much. I will think about what you said about forgiveness."

Mrs. Samuelson was waiting for her when she arrived. Charlene said, "I stopped by to visit with Pastor Jones. I am sorry I am late. If it is all right with you, I will stay later today to make up for the time I missed."

With a wave, Mrs. Samuelson said, "That is all right, child. I am sure you needed to visit with him. Are you, alright? You look a little down in the mouth today. What is wrong?"

Charlene told her about her daddy unexpectedly coming back to town, entering their home while they were away from home, leaving his things, and so forth. She told her all about the ruckus he had caused last night, including the policemen coming to help them, and about how upsetting the whole thing has been.

Then she said, "Pastor Jones said we must forgive him, or we will continue to carry around all that hurt and bitterness and never get over what he has done to us."

Mrs. Samuelson sat with a troubled look on her face, hands folded, and then slowly nodded. "Yes, my child, forgiveness is the only way to ever heal. Even though the human side of us wants to do something else in retaliation, the best thing to do is forgive. Now, forgiveness doesn't necessarily happen overnight. But if you pray to God, He will help you overcome what has happened to your family. Yes, it is the only way. Oh my! Where are my manners? Would you like something cold to drink?"

Charlene smiled at her and said, "Just ice water please. I need to get to work and make up for my tardiness.

"But first, did I tell you about working in the hospital lab? I am earning extra credit. I work there Tuesdays and Thursdays after school. Oh, Mrs. Samuelson, it is the most exciting thing in the world. Dr. Hayden called and asked me whether I would like to shadow a lab tech. It turns out there are a whole team of lab techs. They are just wonderful and so knowledgeable. And you should see all the stuff I have to wear! Goggles, hat, mask, shoe coverings, white lab coat, and gloves. I am sure there must be something else I am forgetting. Anyway, I am to keep a log of time, date, what type of tissue, and cells I have seen. And to list them by name.

"Oh, Mrs. Samuelson, it is almost as much fun as working for you. Now I must get to work. I've talked much too much."

Mrs. Samuelson chuckled merrily.

And with that Charlene grabbed the cleaning supplies and got down to the business of making the house shine. Before she knew it, the first floor was finished. She looked at the checklist on a three-by-five card to make sure she had left nothing out.

Then she asked, "May I bring in some flowers from your garden for a bouquet for the table?"

Mrs. Samuelson was delighted.

With that Charlene asked, "May I have Friday off? That is the prom night."

Mrs. Samuelson said, "Yes, you may if you and Sean will come by my house so I can have a look at you."

Immediately, Charlene threw her arms around her and said, "Oh, thank you. It is a deal."

Mrs. Samuelson hugged her right back. She stood on the front porch and watched an amazing young woman walk down the sidewalk.

Charlene turned and saw her; she flashed a big smile and gave a great, big wave.

Margaret was pacing the floor when Charlene arrived home.

She said, "You are late. I was so worried. After last night's trouble, I was so worried about you."

Charlene told her about going by the pastor's office before going to Mrs. Samuelson's home. That was why she was later than normal.

Margaret asked, "Did you arrange for another box of food to be delivered?"

Charlene replied, "No, I guess I should have. I can do that tomorrow."

Margaret said, "No, this time I will do it. Not receiving that support check has really hurt our grocery money. We are just barely making it on my salary."

There was a loud knock on the front door. Both Margaret and Charlene froze. They looked at one another, then Margaret walked over and moved the curtain a little to look out. It was Pastor Jones. Relieved, Margaret opened the door.

He said, "I was in the neighborhood and thought I would bring this extra box of food that someone placed in my car. I hope you don't mind. Do you have some iced tea? I sure could use a glass."

Margaret was laughing and said, "Please come in. Yes, I have iced tea. Charlene, take this box of precious gold while I pour a glass of iced tea. Please have a seat. It is nice to see you."

The small talk began. He said, "I see you have new neighbors. What do you know about them? Have you invited them to church?"

And so, a pleasant pastoral visit began.

Soon he said, "I have some more stops to make before I get home, so I better run along. I look forward to seeing you in church on Sunday."

Margaret said, "Pastor, thank you for the box of food. It is greatly needed and appreciated."

He looked at her, then at Charlene, and he nodded and said, "You are welcome. Good night."

Margaret turned, clasped her hands together, and said, "Thank You, Lord, for this box of food, for the people who donated it, and for our dear pastor for delivering it to us. Amen."

Charlene was thinking. *One more month of school, but homework still needs to be done. So, get down to work. But two more nights until the prom.* She was so excited about the prom, Sean would look so handsome in a suit. She sat daydreaming, then jerked back to the reality that homework was still waiting.

Chapter 2

♦♦♦

There was so much excitement in the school for juniors and seniors that the teachers may as well have written Friday off. But somehow the school day progressed.

Midafternoon a note from the office was delivered to Charlene. An unsigned message said, "Sean will take you to get your hair fixed right after school. Meet him at the front of the building. Don't be late."

As soon as the dismissal bell rang, Charlene made her way through the mass of hurrying students to the front door.

There Sean was patiently waiting for her.

She said, "How did you get out of class and get out here so fast?"

He answered, "My last class wasn't as far away as yours. Hey, girl, get a move on. We have to get you beautified, like you need any help with that!" He looked at her and smiled broadly.

She said, "Who is paying for my hair appointment?"

He said, "I am sworn to secrecy. Now get in the truck!"

He dropped her off at the hair salon. He had something to do and said he would be back when she was finished.

When he returned to pick her up, he stood with his mouth open as he looked at her. The sides of her long hair were drawn up high across the back of her head and secured with a clip that was the same color as her dress. It secured long curls, which cascaded down to her shoulders. She had also gotten a facial. She wasn't used to wearing very much makeup. For one thing, she couldn't afford it. The makeup lady had softly accentuated her eyebrows, outlined her eyes, and enhanced her eye lashes. Her peaches-and-cream complexion had received a tiny touch of makeup, and her well-shaped lips had benefited from a soft pink gloss.

He looked at her as if he had never seen her before. When he found his voice, he said with emotion, "Charlene, you are gorgeous!"

The hairdresser and makeup lady both surrounded him and said, "Yes, she is. Now go enjoy your prom."

Sean fumbled around for the door handle, trying to open the door for Charlene. But he couldn't take his eyes off her. When they were seated in the pickup, he was still looking at her.

She said, "Now Sean, if we are going to get home safely, you need to look at the road." When she said that, they both laughed.

Before he started the truck, he said, "I am the luckiest guy on the planet to have you for my date."

She reached over and patted his hand, which rested on the steering wheel, and said, "Thank you. And I am feeling very lucky to have you as my date. You know, you are my very first one."

Sean dropped Charlene off at her home. When she was getting out of the truck, she said, "Remember to come get me no less than thirty minutes early. Mrs. Samuelson wants us to come to her house so she can see us. She is so sweet."

Sean waited until she was on the porch before he drove away. He just couldn't tear his eyes away from her. He thought, *she just has no idea how attractive she is. Hmm, that is the same thing I have told my parents.*

In no time at all, it seemed, Sean was standing at her door. When she opened the door, there he stood in a nice suit, white shirt, blue cummerbund, and bow tie. He looked so handsome.

She said, "Wow! Is this the same guy who is my lab partner? You look so handsome. I will have to smack off all the girls who will be coming after you."

He started laughing when she said that.

Margaret said, "Wait one second. I want to take a picture of you two."

After that, they walked down the sidewalk, going to the truck—wait! There was no truck. Instead there sat a nice car.

She said, "Where is your truck? I love that truck."

He responded, "I couldn't take a princess in my truck. My daddy let us borrow his car."

By now they were at Mrs. Samuelson's home. Sean hurried around the car to open the door for Charlene. Mrs. Samuelson stood at the door with the biggest smile on her face that you can imagine. They walked up the sidewalk to join her.

She said, "My goodness. Let me look at the two of you. Sean, you are the most handsome guy I have seen in many a day, and look at our little princess. Oh, I wish I was a young person once again so I could see the looks on the faces when you two walk into that room! You are both beautiful. Now go have a good time. And I want to hear all about it! And you better not leave any details out when you tell me about this evening. Now, go, go." She hugged them both and waved goodbye.

When Sean and Charlene walked into the gym, now transformed into a banquet room and ballroom, a disco ball was turning, and music was playing. In one corner, at the front of the gym, an area was set up for prom pictures. They went there and had a series of photographs taken.

Next, they went to look for some of their friends. There was a steady roar of excited voices. All of them were trying to talk louder than the next person. Sean and Charlene walked into a group of their friends and joined in the conversations. All of them were oohing and aahing over each other's dresses and dates. Then they saw Sean and Charlene. They welcomed them into the group.

Someone said, "Some of us are going over to the next town after the prom to spend the night."

Charlene innocently said, "Why? What for?"

Joe said, "Really, Charlene? If you must ask, then maybe someone needs to educate you. What are you—some sort of nun or something?" Then everyone howled with laughter.

Sean guided Charlene away from the group and said, "I am sorry.

But that is all right. It is something some of the students do, but we aren't going. They go over there to drink and then to spend the night in a hotel."

Innocently, Charlene said, "You mean, spend the night together?"

Sean said, "Yes. It is expected among a lot of students."

Charlene said, "Well, count me out of that group! I had no idea. I plan to save myself for my husband on my wedding night. Why would I want to go throw it away like that?"

Someone announced over the loudspeakers that the students should be seated because dinner would be served within a few minutes.

Sean and Charlene made their way to a table and were seated.

Charlene looked at Sean and said, "I hope I didn't embarrass you when I asked why they are going to the next town. I had *no* idea why they would be going."

He said, "That is okay. I hadn't made plans to attend that activity. Some kids are going to drink too much and get into trouble. I do not want to be around when that happens."

Charlene caught his arm, leaned over, and said, "Thank you. I am so proud of you! I don't ever want to disappoint my mother or Mrs. Samuelson, and I think you feel the same way about your parents. Going there would certainly have disappointed all of them."

Soon the table was full of excited students, and the meal was served.

After the meal was over, dance music was playing. Couples got up and began dancing.

Sean looked at Charlene and said, "Want to give it a try?"

She looked at him, smiled, and said, "Yes, let's do it." They both laughed.

Charlene said, "I hope that I do not kill your toes." By the time they reached the dance floor, slow music had begun. Sean held her in his arms, and they began to sway to the music. Charlene was just getting comfortable when the disc jockey kicked the music into a wild, lively, loud beating of drums. The students yelled with glee and began to do some sort of crazy dance Charlene had never seen. A startled Charlene looked up into Sean's laughing face and said, "Oh my goodness. What is that?"

Around midnight the group began to leave. Sean and Charlene headed for home. Sean said, "I have to work tomorrow."

Charlene said, "This weekend I am not working, so I will help my mother with chores around the house."

She looked at Sean and said, "Thank you for inviting me tonight. I had no idea as to what to expect. Thank you again. It was lovely. I hope I didn't cripple you for life by stepping on your toes."

They were soon pulling into Charlene's driveway. Sean turned to Charlene, leaned over, and gave her a little kiss. "Thank you for going with me. I thought I was going to have to hog-tie and drag you to this prom. I hinted every way that I could think of before I finally blurted out that I was asking you out. I hope you will go with me again sometime."

She said, "Thank you. I am sure there will be other opportunities ... but *not* going to the next town to spend the night." And they both laughed.

Sean walked her to the door and kissed her good night. She smiled at him, and they said good night.

The next morning after the prom, Charlene and her mother were cleaning house, doing laundry and all the chores that needed to be taken care of, when the phone rang. It was Sean.

His breathless voice had a catch in it, "Charlene, have you heard the news?"

She said, "No. What's up?"

He gasped out, "There was a bad car wreck last night. There were two cars of students from our high school who had been drinking. They were racing and had a wreck. Some are dead, and some are badly injured. They are some of the kids from our group last night. Charlene, I am so glad we didn't go with them. If we had, that could have been us. Thank you for saying, 'Count me out.' You were so beautiful. I could easily have been persuaded to go if you had agreed."

Charlene asked, "How many are dead?"

He said, "Four are killed, and two are badly injured. One of the badly injured ones is Joe. He is the guy who was so rude to you. This thing really has me shook up. Tonight, there is to be a candlelight vigil at the high school. Will you go with me?"

Charlene agreed. They ended the conversation. Charlene hung up the phone and turned to her mother to tell her what had happened.

Then she said, "I need to call Mrs. Samuelson and let her know we are all right, because she may have heard about the accident. I want her to know that Sean and I didn't go with the group to the next town. I just want her to know that we are all right."

The town had suffered so much over the past three years, and now this senseless, tragic event had occurred. Everyone gathered on the high school lawn. They huddled together to gain strength from one another. People were hugging friends, family and even strangers. Some were angry and crying bitter tears. The area around the flagpole was filled with people. They linked hands and arms, and sang songs as they were striving to find comfort. They cried some more. By now there was a pile of flowers stacked around the flagpole; it seemed to be a makeshift memorial. They held hands and linked arms as Pastor Jones prayed for the living. The dark, soft night air was filled with flickering candlelight reflecting off tear-stained faces. The crowd lingered far into the night, dreading to go home and think of all the what-if questions parents often think as they look at their own children after such a tragedy.

Earlier in the evening, Margaret and Jerimiah were standing near Sean and Charlene. There was a stir in the crowd as someone was talking loudly, saying, "Excuse me. Pardon me. I need to get through. Thank you." Everyone looked around to see what the commotion was all about. It was George. He came to Margaret and Charlene.

He said, as he looked at Charlene, "I heard about the accident, but no names were given. I had to come to see if you are all right. I was so worried. I thought I might have lost you for good." He reached out to Charlene, and she ran into his arms, crying.

She said, "Those kids were in our group. We saw them last night at the prom. We just heard about the tragedy this morning."

George said, "I heard about it on the morning news. I drove all day to get here. That is how I heard about the candlelight vigil. Charlene and Margaret, I am so sorry I made such a mess of things. Please forgive me."

By now Margaret, Charlene, and George were all crying.

George said, "Why does it take something tragic to happen before a person can see what is valuable?"

Rather awkwardly, Charlene introduced George to Sean, and Margaret introduced him to Jerimiah. They all then discussed what had led to the tragic incident leading to the death of four young people.

Around midnight, the crowd began to break up. George said goodbye to everyone and was making his way back to his truck when he turned around and said to Charlene, "I will write you soon. I have a job and will be sending you both money once again. Let me know when you graduate. I would like to attend your graduation." He hugged her and walked away.

Sean took Charlene home. She asked him to join her at church the next day. She said, "Pastor Jones planned to speak on forgiveness, but in light of last night's tragedy, I suspect his subject matter will be different."

Chapter 3

✦✦✦

The service began with a soprano and alto duet; the song was "It Is Well with My Soul." As the last strains of music drifted away, Pastor Jones stood before a packed congregation. He looked out over the audience, hesitated, and then began speaking.

"My brothers and sisters, as you all know, once again our small town has been hit by tragedy. Today I had planned to speak on the subject of forgiveness. But with the tragic events of last night, I have changed my topic.

"Three years ago, the number one industry moved out of town. That resulted in people moving away. Many families who remained were broken apart by crime and poverty. Some families were broken apart by divorce, and the list goes on. These three years, heartaches, pain, and suffering of unimaginable levels have run deep in this community. I had planned to say, 'We need to forgive the business people who brought about all the events that cause the domino effect that almost destroyed our town.' I planned to talk about forgiving all who have wounded us. You see, Mark Twain once said, 'Forgiveness is the fragrance the violet sheds on the heel that has crushed it.'

"You, my brothers and sisters, are a strong people though you have been crushed like the violet. You have rallied together and never stopped moving forward. Emotionally and physically, you have the scars to prove it. You are a strong people. You never failed to hold on to hope. Your faith has been strong, just as the song just sung, which was written by Horatio G. Spafford, who experienced tragic events one after another.

"Despite all he went through, he was able to hold onto his faith and look to God for strength and mercy. Some of the things that happened to him were these: He lost his business. He lost numerous young children and then four daughters who were aboard a ship that sank at sea. Despite all that, he continued to cling to God. So must we. He wrote that song when he was aboard another ship near the place where his daughters had died. Yet he wrote, 'It is well with my soul.'

"We in Wilsonville have yet another mountain to climb with the senseless death of four high school students and the serious injuries of two others, whose lives are forever changed. Adults and young people, if you do not learn anything else by this tragedy, I hope you have learned this weekend that you are not invincible. You cannot drink and drive, not to say anything about racing. Along with the pain and suffering the parents, families, and friends are going through this weekend, there is another thing they are dealing with. Anger. Yes, anger is part of the grief process. They are angry at their sons and daughters for doing what they knew they weren't supposed to be doing. Now there are four dead youth and two seriously injured. Parents, families, and friends all have broken hearts. And are saying, 'Why?' Beloved, we do not have the answers to the whys of life. We must have the faith to lean on the breast of our Lord Jesus Christ and let Him carry us through the valleys of the shadow of death. But we as a community will get past this. One day at a time, we will move on. We must depend on God to give us peace and comfort.

"Let's pause and listen to our male quartet as they sing 'Peace in the Valley' by Thomas A. Dorsey.

> I'm tired and weary
> But I must go along
> Till the Lord comes to call me away, oh Lord
> Well, the morning is bright
> And the Lamb is the light

And the night is as far as the day
Oh, there will be peace in the valley for me, for me
There will be peace in the valley for me, oh Lord I pray

"These parents have lost their children. They want young people everywhere to see what happens when humans abuse powerful machines. They have requested to have the two wrecked cars be placed on display on the high school lawn. They have said, 'If this horrific sight will influence even just one student to not drink and drive, then the criticism that we will receive for displaying the destroyed vehicles will be worth it.'

"My brothers and sisters, despite all the pain and suffering we individually and collectively are experiencing, we need to surround these hurting families with our love and support. We must put aside our own pain and minister to these families. Let's come together as a community and enfold them in our arms. When they need to talk, give them your undivided attention. They must learn not only to live without their children but also to forgive their children for what they have done. These parents had hopes and dreams for their children and for their children's future. They are having to say goodbye to those hopes and dreams. Now, along with their children, those hopes and dreams are all gone forever.

"It may seem that these are empty words, but I am going to say them anyway. God's word said, 'I will not put more on you than you can handle.' But, along with that verse, I lean heavily on Philippians 4:13. It says, 'I can do all things through Jesus Christ who strengthens me.' And I will hold on to that promise to get us through this new dark valley in our community.

"God knows what it feels like to lose a child. He gave His only begotten Son to die on the cross for our sins. God's own heart has felt pain and suffering. Jesus felt the pain of sadness when His friend Lazarus died. When He saw His friends Mary and Martha grieving, He wept also.

"During the past three years, our loads have been heavy. Our needs have been great. Many times, our backs have been bent almost to the breaking point, and now another load is added on. But He will not give us more than we can carry. He will be there with us. He may not send another person to help carry your burden, but He will be there with you if you will rely on Him. However, you may be the very thing some hurting person needs when you speak a kind word or lend a helping hand. Put your arms around them and help them carry their burden. Love your hurting neighbor as you love yourself.

"Please stand with me and let us read the Twenty-third Psalm.

> The Lord is my Shepherd;
> I shall not want.
> He makes me to lie down in green pastures;
> He leads me beside the still waters.
> He restores my soul;
> He leads me in the paths of righteousness
> For His name sake.
> Yea, though I walk through the valley
> Of the shadow of death,
> I will fear no evil;
> For you are with me;
> Your rod and Your staff, they comfort me
> You prepare a table before me in the
> Presence of my enemies;
> My cup runs over.
> Surely goodness and mercy shall follow me
> All the days of my life;
> And I will dwell in the house of the Lord forever.
> (NKJV)

"Remain standing as we sing 'Amazing Grace.'"

In closing, the pastor voiced a pray for comfort, safety, and blessings.

Chapter 4

✦✦✦

Monday was a rough day of school for teachers, administrators, and students. Emotions were raw. Extra counselors and clergy trained in counseling were brought in from other school districts and villages to help students with their grief. At the end of the day, Charlene went to Mrs. Samuelson's home to begin her chores.

Mrs. Samuelson was waiting for her. They talked about the prom and the aftermath. Charlene told her the students involved in the wreck had laughed at her because she hadn't been willing to be part of the plans of drinking and spending the night in a hotel. Joe, one of the drivers, had taunted her because of her decision not to go. He wanted to know whether she "was some sort of nun or something."

Mrs. Samuelson said, "Charlene, I appreciated you calling me on Saturday to let me know that you and Sean weren't involved in the car wrecks. So many times, in my long life, I have seen things similar to this tragic event. Every time my heart freezes when I hear it. When I was young, someone I loved very, very much died in a drowning accident. He was swimming in an area he wasn't supposed to be in. Breaking rules, no matter how small they seem to be, can be costly. The ripple effect of pain and sorrow touches everyone."

Charlene reached over, gave her a hug, and said, "I am so sorry." The two friends sat in silence for several minutes. Neither said a word, yet both understood what the other was thinking.

Finally, Charlene said, "Mrs. Samuelson, your house is just like our little home. It just will not clean itself. I better get to work."

Mrs. Samuelson smiled and said, "Child, thank you. I needed our little talks. They mean a lot to me. Run along and take care of your chores."

Charlene picked a large bouquet of flowers and placed it in a vase on the kitchen table. She even set Mrs. Samuelson's favorite tea cup beside the flowers. With that she said, "Bye for now. I will see you Wednesday afternoon." She gave Mrs. Samuelson a big hug and left for home.

The week was a heavy one with four funerals; schedules were disrupted. It was very difficult to try to maintain a regular routine with such painful events happening.

Students gathered each day around the smashed cars on the school lawn. They stood quietly and spoke in hushed tones as they processed the gravity of what had happened to their friends.

Charlene received a letter from her daddy with a check in it just as he had promised.

Dear Charlene,

   I have arranged for you to have a car. It is to be delivered to your house within the next few days. With some of this check, why don't you see if you can get into a driver's ed. class? I know it is a late date. Maybe they will have a cancellation, or maybe someone can teach you. Maybe Sean? Sorry about the last-minute stuff. But things have come together for me so I could get a loan to buy you a car. I hope you like it. It is blue. I hope that is all right.
   Write me when you can.

Love, Dad

Immediately, Charlene wrote him a thank-you note.

Dear Dad,

Thank you for the car. Blue is my favorite color, so I know I will love the car. Thanks for giving it to me. It will certainly help me a lot with summer school. Classes are over in the next town. I have received a scholarship for two college courses. They are courses that our high school does not offer, but I need them to get into college. These courses will help prepare me for cancer research, I hope. The blue car will help me very much.

Thank you.

Love,
Charlene

Chapter 5

◆◆◆

Gradually, a new routine was established. Charlene was able to get into a driver's ed. class. Sean was happy to be the licensed driver to ride along with her on her practice drives.

The end of school was only two weeks away. Charlene and Sean were talking about summer activities.

Charlene said, "I am still trying to figure out my summer schedule."

Sean said he also had been trying to figure out his work schedules as well as summer school again this year.

Charlene said, "Summer school?"

He said, "Yes, didn't you know? I am taking the same courses you are. We can drive together to summer school, only now you may not want to ride with me since you have that snazzy blue car." He had a smile a mile wide, and then he laughed aloud.

She said, "You! You have known all this time and didn't tell me." She playfully smacked him on the shoulder. He laughed all the more. "And what do you mean, not want to ride with you? I love that pickup. It has character."

She paused and said, "You have taken summer classes before?"

He said, "Yes, there were things I needed to take that would pertain to genetics, and our school doesn't offer them, so I picked up a course at a time, sort of like you working for the hospital lab for credit. The counselor helped me pick up some extra credits that I would need."

And the two friends joked and planned the next few months.

In the meantime, Charlene continued to go to the hospital lab. They were allowing her to see how many cells and viruses she could identify. Someone was always guiding and correcting her. They were making sure she always had the correct label on a slide. They had pictures of various viruses, infectious diseases, and cells for her to memorize.

She said, "If these things weren't so dangerous, I could say that some of them are pretty—the shapes, forms, and colors. But then I look at what they can do to a person. I quickly change my thoughts about beauty."

She continued to maintain her hourly log and had the supervisor sign off each day. The supervisor said, "Charlene, you have a natural gift. You are very accurate in identifying various cells and viruses. You will do well in this field. I understand that you are going to summer school. If you can work it into your schedule, we would be happy for you to come in a couple of days a week. You are gaining some excellent experience. Think about it and let me know."

Charlene went home and wrote James a letter.

Dear James,

I must tell you what happened after the prom. Several of the students went to a neighboring town to drink, party, and spend the night at a hotel. Two carloads of our friends had been drinking and began racing. The cars crashed, killing four and badly injuring two. Sean and I didn't go with them. They harassed me for asking why they were going over there. Joe asked me, "What are you—some sort of nun?" Anyway, we didn't go with them.

Sean called Saturday morning, telling me what had happened. The parents wanted the wrecked cars to be placed on the high school lawn as reminders to students of what can happen. No one is invincible. (Not even bronco riders.)

Our prom pictures aren't back yet. I will send you one soon. Oh yes, my dad has bought me a car. He came to the candlelight service at the high school. He surprised us. He apologized for what all he had done. I think he is truly sorry. He has a job and is sending support money once again, so Mom and I are going to make it.

I start summer school a week after school is out. Sean is attending the same classes I am. I hope life is going along fine for you.

Your friend always,
Charlene

PS: I saw the Big Dipper the other night and thought of you.

The following week was just a blur. There were the end-of-school-year activities and tests.

Prom pictures had been received. For several families, painful, raw memories were brought back to the surface as the parents looked at their beautiful children, dressed for what was supposed to have been a night to remember.

Chapter 6

♦♦♦

At school, word was received that Joe was now out of intensive care and had been moved into intermediate care. He would likely be there several months. He was in a body cast as well as casts on both badly broken legs and one arm. He would have months of physical therapy after all the casts were removed.

At last the school year was nearing the end. Perhaps the community could begin to heal over the summer months.

George wrote Charlene a letter.

Dear Charlene,

I hope you are able to keep a grip on schoolwork and all you are doing, even with all the pain of the last month. When you have a chance, drop me a note and let me know about the two students who survived the auto crash. Those poor kids have a lot to carry around with them in life.

Tell me, when do you start summer school? How many days a week will you be going? What are you taking? Please keep in touch. Here is some extra gas money for your car.

Love,
Dad

Charlene replied.

Dear Dad,

Classes begin next week. I will be attending them two nights a week. The classes are both very intense. Sean and I are taking the same classes. This way we can ride together and split the cost of gas. Thanks for my car and for the gas money. This has come at a good time.

Joe is out of intensive care and was moved into intermediate care. He is in a body cast. Both legs are in casts, and one arm is in traction. He will be hospitalized at least six months and then will have to have extensive physical therapy. No one has said how Joyce is doing. As far as I know, she is still in the hospital. Joe always made a big splash around school, so everyone discusses his injuries. Joyce was a quiet person and not as well known. When I know something, I will let you know.

Love,
Charlene

The summer months flew by. Now it was time for school to resume. The school counselor had Charlene's educational plan scheduled for her. Again, she and Sean were in the same classes.

She continued working for Mrs. Samuelson and volunteering at the hospital lab. One day when she was at the lab, Dr. Hayden walked in.

He said, "Charlene, I was hoping I would see you. There is someone in the hospital I want you to see. As soon as you finish here, come to my office."

Charlene finished her shift, logged out, had her notebook signed by the supervisor, and made her way down to Dr. Hayden's office. She knocked on the door and was welcomed in.

Dr. Hayden said, "Come with me. There is someone I want you to see."

As they walked down the hallway, he asked about her summer school and the classes she was taking this year. Soon they arrived at a hospital room.

When they entered the room, a very thin, pale young man said, "Charlene!"

Taken back for a moment, Charlene suddenly recognized the person to be Joe. She said, "My goodness! I am so surprised. When did you get into town? I would shake your hand, but frankly I am afraid that I might hurt you."

He laughed, "I guess I do look a mess. But I am so much better than I was there for a while. I asked Dr. Hayden about you. He said that you volunteer in the lab. I asked him if it was all right for you to come see me when you were finished with your assignment. Have you heard how Joyce is doing?"

Charlene said, "No. We have heard nothing. Do you know where she is and how she is?"

Joe replied, "All I heard is, they took her to a specialty hospital for head trauma. I have heard nothing else. They usually change the subject when I ask. Maybe you can find out something more. But I have something else I must say, and this is it.

"What I have to say is rather difficult for a tough guy like me to ever say. But I am *really* sorry I was so rude to you at the prom. Many times, these weeks and months, in my mind I have seen the hurt look on your face when I mocked you, and I have heard my own rude words ring in my own ears. Will you please forgive me? I had no right to do that. The wrecks would never have happened if we had all listened to you.

"Also, when I get out of the hospital and rehab, there is something I want to do. I have not told anyone what I am about to tell you. You are the first to hear this. I want to go to the junior high school and tell the kids to not drink and drive. I want to go to the high school and tell our friends the same thing. I wanted you to know this.

"It means a lot for you to come to see me. Thank you. And again, please forgive me."

Charlene, wiping tears from her face, said, "Joe, of course I forgive you. I would give you a big hug, but I am afraid to even touch you. Anyway, I am proud of you for making plans to visit the two campuses and tell the kids your story. Who knows? You may prevent this from happening to any more Wilsonville students."

The two chatted for a few more minutes. The nurse came in to give Joe his medication, so Charlene excused herself and was turning to leave when she said, "I will stop in again when I am back at the lab."

He smiled and said, "I would really like that."

Charlene went back to Dr. Hayden's office and knocked on his door. He invited her in.

She asked him about Joyce. She said, "I didn't know her very well, just her name. We didn't have any classes together. Her daddy came to Wilsonville to work on the dam."

He looked very troubled. He paused as if searching for the right words to say.

Charlene said, "Joe told me that she had head trauma and was taken to a specialty hospital. Is that true?"

He slowly nodded. He said, "There is more, but Joe must not be told yet. She is on life support. She is classified as brain dead. They are waiting for family to come in from out of state before they unplug her. Whatever you do, do not tell anyone. It will be known very shortly. I have told you this in the strictest of confidences."

Charlene said, "Oh my!" After a long pause, she said, "A doctor certainly carries a heavy load. Sir, I am so sorry I asked. I will tell no one. I will wait for the word … but who will that word come from?"

"As soon as the word is released, rest assured the whole town will know," he said softly. "Information like that spreads fast. Always remember that dying is simply part of the life cycle. You go on home now. Do your homework and continue preparing for your life."

She walked over, patted him on the shoulder, and said, "I will see you next time."

After dinner Charlene settled into the homework routine. She had just completed her assignments when she heard the phone ring.

Her mother answered, and her voiced sounded very excited to be speaking with someone. Then her voice changed, and she said, "Oh no! I am so sorry!" And the conversation continued.

Out of curiosity, Charlene walked into the room where her mother was. She wanted to know what was going on. Then her mother said, "Yes, you can stay with us. We would be delighted to have you. Yes, the den sofa makes into a bed. Yes, yes, oh my, yes. We will be expecting you. I am delighted that you called us. We will look forward to seeing you soon. I am just sorry it is under these circumstances. We will be waiting. Bye."

Margaret turned to Charlene and said, "I have some sad news and some wonderful news. The sad news is, Joyce is to be unplugged from all the life-support equipment tonight. The good news is, James and his parents are here and will be staying with us."

Charlene said, "Whoa! Wait. Did you leave out something? Why are they here? And what connection do they have with Joyce?"

Margaret turned to Charlene and said, "Joyce is James's father's niece. Joyce and her parents moved here so the father could work on the dam. They have not been in Wilsonville very long. Anyway, Joyce is James's cousin. James came with his parents. They will be staying with us. You and I will share my room, and the parents can have yours. James will sleep on the den sofa. It will be so good to see them. But it will be very sad at the same time. We better hurry and get your bed changed and the sofa bed made up. They are about two hours away. Joyce was in some specialty hospital for head trauma. Did you even know Joyce?"

The conversation continued as the two women quickly transformed the house from a house for two to a house for five.

Charlene mused, *I wonder what James is like. I wonder how tall he is.*

Margaret responded, "You better hurry up and get your books and things out of your room and whatever you plan to wear tomorrow. Oh, don't forget your pj's. Oh, Charlene I am so excited to see these dear friends."

Charlene said, "I know. I am excited about seeing them, too. But I am nervous. James has a girlfriend. So, things won't be the same as they were nearly four years ago. Yes, I am very nervous. His girlfriend didn't want him writing to me. Wonder what she will say when he says he stayed with us."

Margaret laughed. She said, "Don't worry about that. It will take care of itself. Right now, concentrate on getting this house company ready."

Charlene cleaned the hall bathroom and laid out a stack of fresh towels. They had no sooner finished the last detail when a car pulled into the driveway.

Chapter 7

◆◆◆

Margaret and Charlene rushed to the front door. It looked so natural to see that family of three walking up the sidewalk, only James was as tall as, or taller than, his father. *What's with that?* Charlene couldn't believe her eyes. Everyone was hugging and laughing and saying how good it was to see one another. Margaret expressed her sympathies and invited them into the house.

Charlene turned to James and said, "Look at you! You didn't tell me that you are as tall as your dad."

Mr. Walters turned around and quickly responded, "Wait one minute, young lady! He isn't as tall as I am—yet. I still have a *quarter* of an inch on him." And everyone was laughing.

Charlene said, "James, do you want to go sit on the porch and let the adults talk?" That seemed like an agreeable plan.

When they walked outside, Charlene said, "Look! There is the Big Dipper!" They discussed that for a few minutes. Then Charlene asked, "Will your girlfriend be upset with you for staying at our house?"

James responded, "Oh no. We broke up. She was too clingy. What about Sean? Will he be upset?"

Charlene said, "We aren't dating. We rode to summer school, and this being a small school, we have the same classes. No, he won't be upset at all. We are just very good friends." Changing the subject, she said, "I didn't know Joyce was your cousin. I didn't have any classes with her. She seemed nice, was very quiet. I just knew who she was. If I had known she was your cousin, I would have made more of an effort to get to know her. Now, tell me about you. Did your collarbone heal all right?"

James seemed relieved at the change of topic.

He said, "Yes, it is healed. I am not riding right now. I've been too busy with school. There seems to be a little next-door-neighbor girl who thinks she is going to beat me. You said that I didn't say how tall I had gotten. Well, you didn't tell me how beautiful you have gotten. When we pulled up into your driveway, I was expecting that little tomboy next-door-neighbor girl to come bouncing out the door. Then you appeared. Wow! I was blown away."

Charlene laughed at him. She said, "You are too funny!" She paused and then continued, "Listen to our parents. Have you ever heard such chatter? I just wish things had gone differently and that my dad was here. Then it would be a perfect evening. Don't you think we need to go back inside?"

He said, "Wait. Tell me about the people living in our house. Did they take down the tree house?"

Charlene replied, "They are a very nice retired couple. They are Mr. and Mrs. Johannsson. No, they didn't take down the tree house. Wait until you see it. Mr. Johannsson repaired, painted, and expanded it. It is some fancy place now. They have grandchildren who love that tree house. You will be amazed."

James said, "One more thing. Do you still want to meet when we turn twenty-one?"

Quickly Charlene replied, "Sure, don't you? Or have you changed your mind?"

He said, "No, I haven't changed my mind. After being back here, now after seeing you, already I don't want to leave, but I know I will have to."

Charlene mused, *"Four years of college will keep us crazy busy.* Do you know where you want to go to college? I've contacted Baylor, Rice, University of Houston, as well as some others in the Midwest, plus Johns Hopkins and Duke University. Sean and I have applied at the same schools. I know—dreams and wishes, wishes and dreams. May as well dream big. But I know I will need some major scholarships to attend any of those schools. They are all close to good med schools. I'm planning into the future. I am aware that in three or four years, I will have to apply for med school, and I hope I get accepted by one of my choices. Who knows? First, we have to get through the first four years."

James said he was thinking of some of the midwestern and western colleges. He had sent in several applications. "Now for the waiting game."

Charlene teasingly said, "After all of that talk, see how fast four years will go by. With you here on the porch tonight, it is like you have never been away."

James said, "I agree. I was thinking the same thing."

"Have you thought more about what you want to major in?" queried Charlene.

"Yes, I want to be a vet. I want to work with large animals. Charlene, I wish you could come out to Idaho and see that beautiful country. And I want you to see my horses. I love those big beasts."

She answered, "That would be fun. I have tried to visualize what it looks like. I even read books at the library on Idaho. It must be an amazing place to live."

He said, "Would you consider concentrating your search more on midwestern colleges? Maybe we could get into the same school. I would really like that."

She said, "Hmm, now there is a thought. Hmm, yes, I guess I could. So long as they come up with some very big scholarships. I am working myself crazy trying to maintain a high-grade point average to give myself a chance in the scholarship area. I am not sure where I am in class ranking. I don't want to know until the very end of school. I don't want to stress myself out."

She paused and then added, "I have really missed you. I wouldn't have admitted it three or four years ago, but I really depended on you to pull me along and challenge me. After you left, I had to challenge myself. It was easier when you were here and constantly pushing and dragging me along. I guess Sean sort of filled that void. He challenges me as much or more than you did. Can you believe that?"

James chuckled and said, "I need to tell him he has created a monster because now you are pushing me. When your letters would come and you would tell what all you were doing, it made me work harder. It was just like in the old days when the little next-door-neighbor girl was challenging me, making better grades than me. *Bruising my ego.* Then I would score higher than you on a test. Then you would wax me on the next test. Remember those days? I miss those days. If you went to the same college with me, then we could study together. We could keep one another on target—me with my vet school and you in research … Those have been our dreams a long time, Charlene. Let's make them happen!"

Rising to her feet, Charlene said, "I like that idea. Do you want anything to eat or drink? Please forgive my bad manners. We have been so busy talking that I forgot to ask. I just got carried away. I was so excited to see you."

James stood beside her, just admiring the good-looking next-door-neighbor girl. Then he said, "Sure, let's go get something. Is there a fast-food place close by?"

Charlene said, "Let me get my car keys. There is a Dairy Queen a few blocks over."

The two went back into the house and asked their parents whether they could bring them something from DQ.

Mrs. Walters said, "Nothing for me. I am thinking all I want is a hot shower and bed. Today has been a long day." Mr. Walters voiced a similar response.

Margaret just said, "No, thank you."

The two friends drove to the Dairy Queen, placed their orders, and resumed their conversations.

Sean came through the door. He said, "I thought that was your car. I just got off work and was heading home when I saw that little, blue machine."

Charlene said, "Hi, Sean. This is James. Do you remember each other from eighth grade? Sean, Joyce was James's cousin. I didn't know she was related to James. Did you?"

The guys shook hands, and Sean sat in a chair beside them.

James said, "So this is the Sean who has been challenging Charlene in all her classes. We three have been competing in class since we were first-graders. I can't believe we are still talking about Charlene challenging someone. She is *still* at it."

Nodding, Sean said, "Yes, she is still at it. And wrong about me challenging her. I think it is the other way around. She may not be very big, but she is powerful. Never underestimate her. She is tough for an ol' girl."

James shot back, "You are telling me? We were next-door neighbors all our lives until my family moved away. She has a way of making you eat her heel dust. Just tell *me* about her challenging you."

And the guys continued their banter and teasing Charlene like two big brothers would do.

The three friends had a happy conversation going until it was closing time for Dairy Queen.

The guys shook hands and said, "See you next time."

Driving home, James said, "While you are at school tomorrow, I will be working on my assignments from school. My teachers gave me a list of assignments to complete while I am out of school."

Charlene gave him her schedule for the following day. After school, she would be working two hours at the hospital lab. She said, "Mother will be at work. I'll be at school. You should have a quiet house to work in, unless you go work in the tree house."

And so, the reunion of two old friend had begun.

Chapter 8

◆◆◆

Charlene left for school. Margaret left for work. Mr. and Mrs. Walters went to his sister's house to help her make funeral arrangements. James had the house to himself. He buckled down, trying to take care of as many assignments as possible during the time alone.

By eleven o'clock, he felt he needed to stretch his legs and get some fresh air before resuming the last assignment for the day. He decided to go visit the next-door neighbors, Mr. and Mrs. Johannsson.

When he knocked on the door, a pleasant older lady answered the door. She said, "Yes, may I help you?"

He introduced himself and said he had been raised in that house. They had bought the house from his parents. He asked, "Would it be possible for me to see the tree house? The little next-door-neighbor girl and I used to spend hours playing in that tree house."

Mrs. Johannsson called to her husband. Soon a friendly man appeared at the door. Introductions were made again. James explained that he would like to see the tree house, if that would be all right. He explained that he and the little next-door-neighbor girl used to play in that house.

Mr. Johannsson chuckled and said, "James, have you seen that little next-door-neighbor girl?" Then he said, "Oh my! That girl will be a knockout by the time she is grown. And I hear she is one super-intelligent student, too."

James replied, "I know something about her being a sharp student.

Charlene and I have been in competition our whole lives. If I scored higher on a test than she did, the next test she would cream me. Oh yes, I have firsthand knowledge of how well she does in school." Everyone laughed.

"She wants to be a cancer research scientist, and I plan to be a vet working with large animals, preferably horses."

Mrs. Johannsson said, "My, my. Come in and visit with us. Let me show you the house. Which was your room? Tell me some more about you and Charlene. I was just making sandwiches. Will you join us for lunch?"

Mr. Johannsson said, "I want to get my two bits in sometime. I want to show you the tree house. Our grandchildren love it. I sort of got carried away and added onto it. It looks somewhat like a Swiss chalet now."

And so the midday drop-in visit went. There was laughing, old childhood stories told about the little girl next door, and talk of the downsizing of the town, people moving away, and so forth. And, of course, James told them about his new life in Idaho, living on a horse ranch, and his newfound love for horses. Soon two o'clock was showing on the clock. James quickly thanked the Johannssons for lunch, for allowing him to see the tree house, and for welcoming him into their home. He had enjoyed his visit. He said goodbye and dashed back across the yard to finish his schoolwork. He dare not miss any assignment!

After school was out for the day, Charlene went to the lab. She felt at home among all the test tubes, slides, microscopes, white coats, masks, and so forth. She constantly asked questions and wrote the questions and answers in her notebook. She was introduced to new microorganisms. After her two hours were completed, she asked the supervisor, "May I study in one of the offices? We have houseguests at our house who are in town for Joyce's funeral. There is no place for me to study. I shouldn't take up your space but for an hour or so. I promise to not be a distraction."

She was given permission. The supervisor helped her set up a quiet area, where she could study. After she completed her last assignment, she tiptoed out the door with a quick wave to the lab techs.

When she reached home, Charlene's mother said, "I was about to get worried about you."

Charlene said, "I worked in the lab today. I stayed a little over time. James, what did you do today?"

He told her about his interesting visit with Mr. and Mrs. Johannsson. He talked about seeing the tree house and having lunch with them. Then he recounted many of their conversations, but he left out much of what he had said about Charlene.

After supper, Charlene said, "James, would you like to go out to see the progress on the dam? It is amazing to see how they build a layer at a time with rebar and concrete or whatever that mixture is."

He gladly accepted.

There was a parking lot above the work site down in the valley. They could see the strong floodlights erected around the hills on each side of the dam. They could see trucks and men working. From where the little blue car was parked, the men and trucks looked very small.

James shared about when the funeral would be held and said they would probably stay part of the weekend and then head for Idaho. He said, "I know we have to get back to our life on the ranch and back to high school, but I dread leaving again."

In a soft voice, almost a whisper, Charlene said, "I know. When you left the other time, I stood in the street, waving until the moving truck could no longer be seen. I cried my eyes out. I was afraid you would never come back. I thought you would just forget all about me. You have no idea how thrilled I was when I received that first letter from you. I danced around the kitchen, saying, 'He wrote to me. I was afraid he had forgotten all about me.'"

James said, "That wasn't about to happen. The little next-door-neighbor girl had gotten into my head. I wasn't about to forget her." He leaned across, caught her in his arms, and kissed her. They both lingered over that unhurried kiss.

Charlene said, "James, I had thought about this happening sometime and wondered what it would be like to be kissed by you.

All I can say is—" By then James held her tightly and kissed her one more time. He said, "Little next-neighbor girl, I plan to marry you one day." And he kissed her again.

A night guard drove up beside them and visited with the two-young people. He said, "That is quite a sight, isn't it? Just think. A couple or three months ago, that was all woodlands and rocks. It won't be long until that cleared area will be covered by water. Are you two from around here?"

Charlene said, "Yes, I live here. This is my friend James, who used to live here before the plant closed. He now lives in Idaho and is back for his cousin's funeral. Her dad works here at the dam."

The guard said, "Yes, I know her dad. We are all sad about his loss."

James asked, "When will the dam be completed?

The guard answered, "It should be completed in about three years. It is providing a lot of people with jobs. This project is helping to turn our community around financially." Then he said, "Have a good evening. I need to make the rest of my rounds."

Charlene answered back, "We are leaving also. I have school tomorrow. You have a good evening too."

When they were driving back into town, Charlene said, "Did you really mean what you said?"

James replied, "I meant it with all my heart. I don't know how or when, but we will make it happen. I just know that I want to marry you. I hope you feel the same way about me. I am in love with the little next-door-neighbor girl."

Charlene whispered, "James, I have been crazy about you for years. Yes, I care a lot for you. I am not sure how we can make all this come together. First, we must get through the things happening right now. I am going to miss you so much when you go back home. I wish I didn't have to go to school tomorrow, but I must."

He replied, "I will be busy. Don't worry about that. Tomorrow evening we can be together again. I've been thinking. Maybe we can work out getting together over the Christmas holidays. That would be something to think about."

Chapter 9

✦✦✦

After school the next day, Charlene drove home to get James. She said, "Today is my day to work for Mrs. Samuelson. I want you to meet her. You can drop me off after our visit and come back and get me, if that is okay with you." As they were pulling up in front of the house, she said, "This is where I work Mondays, Wednesdays, and Fridays. I want you to meet her and vice versa."

Charlene was getting ready to knock on the door when Mrs. Samuelson opened the door. Smiling, she said, "My goodness, child. Who is this handsome young man?"

Charlene replied, "I have someone I want you to meet. Remember, I mentioned that my best friend had moved to Idaho? Well, here he is. This is James. We have known each other our entire lives. I wanted you to meet him. He and Joyce are cousins. James and his parents are in town for Joyce's funeral."

Mrs. Samuelson said, "Oh James, I am so sorry for your family's loss. My goodness. Come in this house. James, I am so happy to meet you. You must be some sort of special person from the times Charlene has talked about you. I understand you are an excellent student and plan to be a vet. Is that true?"

Not meeting Mrs. Samuelson's gaze, he said, "I try to keep up with Charlene. She has given Sean and me a run for our money all these years. You wouldn't think a little girl her size could be so competitive." And they all laughed.

Mrs. Samuelson said, "Well, I am indeed honored that Charlene would bring you by to introduce you to me."

"James is taking my car on home while I do my chores. Then he will come back and pick me up."

Shifting from one foot to the other, James said, "It was very nice meeting you. Charlene's letters are full of 'Mrs. Samuelson said this and that, and Mrs. Samuelson did that.' I will be back in about two hours to get you, Charlene."

Mrs. Samuelson said, "I can see why you are so fond of him. Now, today will be different from other days when you have been here. Oh well, what can I say? Charlene, today's plans have changed. I am feeling very melancholy. The household chores can wait. I have something I want to share with you and tell you a little bit about my life before you met me. Would you like an iced tea or a bottle of Coke? Thank you for bringing your special friend to meet me. That really means a lot to me. He certainly seems nice."

Charlene accepted a tall iced tea. Together they walked into the kitchen, where a large photo album lay on the big, round antique table.

With a misty look in her eyes, Mrs. Samuelson began to tell her story.

"This house was my home when I was a child." Sweeping her hand around, she continued, "These walls have known many happy times and then heartbreaking times. There were the special times when Mama, Papa, and my sister were here. Mama always wore a clean, starched, and ironed apron over her pretty dresses. Papa smoked his pipe, though most of the time it wasn't lit. Aw, those were happy times. There were lots and lots of laughter. This was a happy house. People were always dropping by to sit on the porch and visit. Mama always had a fresh-baked cake and a pitcher of tea or lemonade, just in case someone dropped by.

"My sister, Jolene, and I had a dollhouse and all the furniture. Papa had made it for us. Look! Here is a picture of us playing with our dollhouse. And these are pictures of my family."

She kept turning page after page and explaining who each of the people were. Then she stopped and said, "This is the last picture

I have of Jolene. She caught scarlet fever and died. Then it was just Mama and Papa and me. We tried very hard to make it a happy home once more, but everywhere we looked, there was a reminder of Jolene. Despite of all that, time went by as it seems to always do. I graduated from high school and went to college. Like you I made good grades. I found a real love for science, much as you have. I graduated from college and began teaching science in our high school here in Wilsonville. It was there that I met this handsome man. His name was George Hamilton Samuelson." She carefully turned a page in the album to a picture of a very handsome man, and she tenderly ran her fingers over the face that was smiling back at her.

"We were married and had two precious children—a boy, Jimmy; and a little girl, Janelle. They were just toddlers when World War II broke out, and my husband was called to join the military. The children started school after my husband entered the navy. Those were very difficult days. Anyway, I continued teaching to support our family. George became a pilot in the navy. He was stationed on an aircraft carrier. They weren't as sophisticated as today's ships. We wrote almost every day. It was such a joy when the white envelopes, trimmed in red, white, and blue, would arrive. His letters didn't require stamps. They were free since he was in the military.

"He was flying in the South Pacific when he was shot down. He was captured by the Japanese. Soon his letters stopped coming. I still have them. The last letter was written the day before he boarded his airplane and was shot down. He was classified as missing in action. The government couldn't say whether he was dead or alive, because they really didn't know.

"Months and years went by. The government could give me no information, though I did continue to receive an allotment check just as if he were alive. Then, when the war was over and prisoners of war were being released, I watched and waited, thinking he would come walking through the door one day. I contacted other men who had been prisoners of war. I kept hoping someone could tell me something about George."

Charlene asked, "Did you ever hear anything?"

Mrs. Samuelson said, "Yes, in 1959 I received a letter saying George's remains had been located, and he was being shipped home. He is buried in our family plot at the Wilsonville cemetery. At last our family had closure. My precious George had come home."

There was a long, painful period of silence as Mrs. Samuelson regained her composure.

Charlene said, "I am so sorry. I shouldn't have asked."

Mrs. Samuelson said in a soft, scolding voice, "Yes, you should, or I would have told you myself. Your question showed that you care. Anyway, Papa became ill and died. The children and I moved back into this house to be with Mama. And I continued teaching.

"My children were good kids. They kept Mama and me very busy. Though they were good students, it took Mother and me a lot of stress-filled hours trying to keep Jimmy focused on his schoolwork. Jimmy was less interested in schoolwork and more focused on having a good time. Jimmy was the curious sort—always exploring and frequently doing things he shouldn't do. We tried to monitor his whereabouts as best we could. But when a kid decides to circumvent rules, they will find a way to do so.

"When he was seventeen, he and a group of young people went to the 'Bottomless Blue Hole' over in another county. Young people for generations have been told not to go there. The land owners had No Trespassing signs up everywhere, and they would call the sheriff anytime that young people were seen sneaking in to swim in the Blue Hole. Jimmy and a group of young students skipped school one day and went to the Blue Hole. Unfortunately, Jimmy drowned. It was impossible to protect him from himself. He was a strong-willed child who was determined to do things his own way.

"My beautiful family, which had begun with a handsome husband and two precious babies, was down to just Janelle, Mama, and me. We were devastated." She took a deep breath, then sighed and shook her head as if still having trouble believing what had happened to her family.

She continued, "Mama lived just a few more years. Janelle graduated from high school and then went off to college. She was strong in math and science. She obtained a degree in math and a teaching certificate."

Charlene asked, "Really? Where does she teach?"

Mrs. Samuelson's reaction showed surprise. Then she said, "Why, child, she is your trig teacher. Didn't you know that she is my daughter?"

A startled Charlene responded, "No! I had no idea that Mrs. Jacobson is your daughter. And I have taken several of her classes. Oh, my goodness! I just know her as Mrs. Jacobson." Then both Mrs. Samuelson and Charlene laughed heartily.

The very next page was devoted to Janelle and husband, John, and their family of four children. Page after page of happy smiling people. Soon Mrs. Samuelson reached the end of the photo album.

She said, "Thank you for indulging an old lady. Today would have been Jimmy's birthday."

Charlene responded, "Thank you for telling me some of your story. No wonder you have been so understanding and compassionate when tragic things have happened in our town these past four years. Thank you for sharing your family with me. And you have a talented daughter. She is an excellent teacher. I bet she is just like you were when you were teaching in our school. I sure didn't know that she is your daughter. Does Sean know she is your daughter? I'll bet everyone else knows except me, and I hadn't put all the pieces together. Next question. Your grandchildren—what grades are they in? Do I know them?"

Mrs. Samuelson said, "You wouldn't know her children. She married later in life, so her children are younger than you. Her oldest is in middle school."

"What an exciting day this has been! I am so happy you shared your photo album with me. What a remarkable story you have shared with me," Charlene said.

They were both silent for a few minutes. Then Charlene continued, "Joyce's funeral is Saturday. James and his parents have been staying with us. They will be heading back to Idaho this weekend. Mrs. Samuelson, I am going to miss him so much when they leave. During these past days, it has been as if they have never been away. James and I are sort of in love and might marry someday. We have been writing ever since they moved to Idaho.

"I am not sure how our futures are going to work out. We are both determined to go to college. It just depends on where we can get scholarships. I have applied to several colleges and universities in the Midwest, East Coast area, and Southwest. So, has James and Sean. Life is very confusing and exciting at this current stage. So much preparation and planning and not wanting to make a misstep. I will look to you for guidance and your wisdom. Mrs. Samuelson, you are my *other* special friend. Thank you for your example and encouragement."

The conversation was interrupted when there was a knock at the door, and there stood James.

Charlene stood up, gave Mrs. Samuelson a big hug, and said, "Thank you for a special afternoon."

Chapter 10

✦✦✦

Joyce's funeral was very similar to that of the other four accident victims. A sorrowing community once again gathered around a hurting family. Everyone knew Joe was still in the hospital and suffering guilt along with feeling sorrow. They knew he would have that to live with for the rest of his life. It is a weighty thing to be the lone survivor. Charlene thought, *What the crowd doesn't know is, he plans to visit middle and high schools and talk to students, warning them about what can happen when you drink and drive recklessly.*

Charlene, Margaret, Jerimiah, and Sean sat together. Charlene kept thinking about James and his parents' plan to leave early Sunday morning. Her heart was heavy just thinking about that. She also thought, *During the past four years, this is the sixth funeral for young people that I have attended … yes, six, counting little Peter.* Again, her mind wandered. *Little Peter, I am working hard to fulfill my promise to you. I am trying to prepare myself for college to help scientists battle cancer. Each time we find something that will kill a cancer cell, I will say, "This one is for you, little Peter."*

Margaret tapped Charlene on the arm. That was when she realized everyone was standing while the casket was about to be wheeled down the aisle. Embarrassed, she quickly joined her mother, standing in respect of Joyce and her family as they walked out, following the casket. She looked at James. He was so tall and handsome. Even at this sad time, her heart still did a flip-flop when their eyes met.

James and his parents spent the evening with Joyce's family. They returned to Charlene's house late in the evening.

They had done their packing for the trip back to Idaho. After breakfast the next morning, they would once again be saying goodbye. Charlene dreaded when they would back out of the driveway. She knew she would once more have a big hole in her heart.

James hugged her tight and said, "I will write." He gave her a quick kiss, ducked his head, and hesitantly got into the car. He kept looking back, and Charlene was waving as they drove down the street.

Charlene turned to her mother and said, "Why does life have to hurt so badly?" She went to her room and wrote a letter to her daddy.

Dear Daddy,

I know I am too old to be calling you Daddy, but at this moment, I would like to be five years old once more, climb up on your lap, and have you fold me safe in your arms. I need to find a safe place that doesn't have pain seeping in through the cracks.

Yesterday was Joyce's funeral. Since you have been gone, there have been six funerals for young people. I am counting little Peter in that six.

James and I picked up right where we left off before they moved to Idaho. It felt for a while like they had never been away. Just now, once more, I stood and watched them drive down the street and out of sight. Why do people I love drive down the street and disappear from my life?

James and I talked about attending the same college or university. That way we could challenge and keep one another on target. He wants to be a vet, and you already know I want to go into cancer research. Anyway, I told him that it depends on what kind of a scholarship I can get as to where I go to school.

And he sort of wants me to come to see him over Christmas break. I am not sure I can manage to do that or even if I want to go in the wintertime. He also said he wants to marry me someday. Dreams and wishes, wishes and dreams!

We have agreed that when we turn twenty-one years of age, we will come back to Wilsonville and meet at the park in the gazebo on the Fourth of July. Again, wishes and dreams.

Well, Daddy, thanks for listening to me tonight. I needed someone to talk to.

Oh yes, I am taking good care of my car. It is called "the little blue machine." Big smile!

Love you, Daddy.
Charlene

Even after the emotional upheaval of the early morning, Margaret and Charlene went to church, as was their custom. When they went to their pew, Jerimiah and Sean were already seated and waiting for them.

When Charlene sat down, Sean slid over beside her and said, "Jerimiah is taking all four of us out to lunch. He hopes that will cheer up you and your mom. He said you and your mom are both sad about your friends leaving for Idaho and need some cheering up. He is really a nice guy." He gave her one of his big, infectious smiles.

About that time the pastor began speaking.

After church Jerimiah said he knew of a family-run restaurant out in the country and thought that would be a nice place to have lunch. When the foursome entered the small restaurant, it was packed with after-church families. The place was filled with wonderful smells of country cooking: chicken fried or grilled steaks, fried chicken, chicken and dumplings, fried catfish, pot roasts, corn on the cob, collard greens, coleslaw, green beans, mashed potatoes, gravy, homemade bread, and on and on the food list went.

Each table had a red-and-white-checkered tablecloth. Friendly waitpersons were standing by with pitchers full of sweet iced tea.

Then Charlene's eyes caught sight of a glass case full of beautiful pies with meringue stacked high and with toasted-brown tipped peaks alongside triple-layered-cakes. A sign on the case said, "Homemade ice cream available."

Charlene and Margaret forgot how sad they had been.

Charlene turned to Jerimiah and with eyes wide said, "This is a wonderful place. I could give you a big hug."

He laughed and said, "I will take that hug," as he reached over and folded her into his arms. He said, "I am so happy you like it. Sean and I thought this was a good idea."

Smiling, Charlene turned to Sean and said, "Thank you, too."

The foursome talked and stuffed their bellies full of the delicious southern, farmhouse cooking; and they topped it off with various desserts, including homemade ice cream.

When they were seated in the car, Jerimiah said, "I have something else I want to show you. We are going for a little drive."

After several minutes of driving, they pulled into a long, winding driveway up to a beautiful home set on a high hill and surrounded by large trees. He drove into the circular driveway, parked at the front door, and invited everyone to follow him.

Everyone was asking, "Who lives here? What are you doing? Jerimiah, do you know these people?"

Jerimiah walked up to the door, took a key from his pocket, and opened the door. He entered the house, turned, smiled, and said, "Come on in. It is okay. This is my house. I just bought it. It is mine."

He looked at Margaret, then at Charlene, and said, "Charlene, I have asked your mother to marry me. If you will give us your blessings, this will be our new home."

A startled and speechless Charlene stood looking from one to the other of the happy couple. Once she found her voice, she said, "Seriously? Are you *really* serious? This is not a joke? Of course, I give you my blessings!"

She reached out to hug them.

She looked at Sean, and he was smiling that big, handsome grin as if to say, *I knew it before you did.*

Jerimiah took them on a tour of the house and grounds. He held Margaret's hand. Sean stood to one side with a very intense look on his face as he watched Charlene. She saw him and, brushing back windblown hair from her eyes, said, "What?"

He grinned that infectious grin and said, "Oh, nothing." He put his hands in his pockets and sauntered away, looking out over the valley below.

Several days went by. Wedding plans were in the making, and excitement was in the air. The wedding would occur around Christmas.

One day when Charlene came home, a letter was waiting for her from her daddy.

Dear Charlene,

Thank you for your letter. I too wish you were five years old again and I could have a "redo" of my life. Every day I regret what I did. But since I can't go back in time, I will make the most of my future by giving you a bit of fatherly advice.

Be aware that James may have been caught up in the emotional moment alone with you. And if no one has told you this, you are one beautiful young lady. If he was caught up in the moment and goes back to Idaho, he may rethink what he said. Please don't think that because he said, "One day I want to marry you," that is what he will feel when he gets back home. It may be nothing but just dreams and wishes when he said it. What I am saying is this: please don't hang your star on that one little sentence. He is young and may get sidetracked with things and people in his own school and neighborhood. One day when you are an adult, you will look back and understand what I am saying.

I tend to agree with you about not going to Idaho in the winter, unless you are planning on doing winter sports. You would fly into Spokane, Washington, and drive to near Coeur d'Alene, Idaho. That country is unbelievably beautiful. The winters can be harsh. Like I say, if you are going for winter sports, mountains near there have nice ski slopes. But a girl from our part of the nation is not used to that cold; nor do you have clothing suitable for that weather. Maybe you can go there another time of the year.

Also, when people go down your street and disappear from your view, it doesn't mean they are out of your life forever. I want to be part of your life for the rest of my life. Due to current circumstances, it will have to be brief visits, letters, and phone calls, but you are forever my little girl.

Love always,
Daddy

Chapter 11

✦✦✦

Charlene hadn't heard from James since he returned to Idaho, so she wrote him a letter.

Dear James:

I hope you and your parents had a nice trip home. When you were here, it almost felt like you had never been away. Now, it feels like you were never here. The days and weeks are going by in a predictable way, as if preprogrammed. However, there is one bit of news. Mother and Jerimiah are getting married over Christmas break. Jerimiah has bought a supercool house out in the country. It is a large house on a hill, with trees all around. As you look down into the valley, there is a magical and peaceful view below. When I looked at that view, I got the feeling there were no problems in the world. I felt at complete peace. When you have a chance, drop me a note.

Your friend forever,
Charlene

The scheduled work day at Mrs. Samuelson's home arrived, and there was so much to tell her dear friend. Of course, there was the latest news about wedding plans.

Mrs. Samuelson asked whether she had heard from James since he returned to Idaho. The answer was no.

Mrs. Samuelson said, "Try not to be too disappointed in your friend. He may have changed more than you thought he had. I just don't want you to be too upset if you learn he used pretty words. Pretty words can be very empty and leave a lot of pain in their wake."

Charlene completed her chores to perfection, as was her pattern. She brought in a bouquet of flowers for the table. She tried to do some extra things that would make Mrs. Samuelson happy. Soon it was time to head for home. Mrs. Samuelson's words kept sounding an alarm in Charlene's mind.

Just before she walked out the door, the phone rang. It was Sean. He wanted to talk with her. He said, "I am going to the hospital to see Joe. Would you like to join me?"

She replied, "I will be happy to visit Joe. Sure, I will meet you there. I have not seen him since before Joyce passed away. I'll see you in a few minutes."

Mrs. Samuelson said, "That Sean is as solid as they come. Be careful, child. I hope you do not have a broken heart over James. I'll see you on Wednesday."

Sean was waiting at the entrance to the hospital when Charlene parked "the little blue machine" next to his pickup. She walked up to greet him, and Sean gave her one of those famous smiles. Together they walked down the hallway, chatting away. When they entered Joe's room, a tired and older-looking young man met their gaze.

They simultaneously said, "Hi, Joe." Then everyone laughed.

Sean said, "I'll bet we could never do that again!"

They walked to Joe's bedside. He still had casts and various pieces of equipment attached to him.

Joe said, "Charlene, I knew when you didn't come back to see me that things weren't good for Joyce. Then I heard you had houseguests from Idaho, and then I heard about the funeral."

Charlene said, "Joe, I am so sorry. I learned we were having houseguests when I got home after visiting with you. It was then that I learned the rest of the story about Joyce. I didn't know she and James were cousins. I hardly knew Joyce. I thought about you but didn't know how to come back here and tell you what I had just learned myself. I felt helpless. I figured the doctors and nurses would tell you. They are more equipped to share that type information. Who told you and when?"

"Since you didn't come back that day, I demanded that someone tell me something. It was then that the doctors came in and told me. They said they had told you not to tell me she was on life support and that they were going to unplug her. I just wanted someone to tell me something. I am the only one left. I look at myself and say, 'Lord, why didn't you take me too?'"

Charlene said, "Joe, I am so sorry. I would never hurt you under any circumstances. I am sorry that I have wounded you. I really didn't know that you were expecting me to come back that night. I didn't know about the rest of the story until about seven o'clock that night when we got the phone call that James and his parents were coming to our house. I guess my mother may have known earlier, but she hadn't told me." Emotionally shaken, Charlene continued. "This week has been one wild and crazy week. I am not making excuses. I am sorry if I have offended you. Is there someone I can call to come be with you?"

Joe replied, "No, having you and Sean here is what I needed."

Charlene walked to his bedside and lay her hand on his shoulder. She thought that was the safest place to make contact without causing physical pain.

Sean asked, "Is there anyone at high school you would like to come for a visit? Charlene and I can circulate the word. I think everyone is afraid to come for a visit because they don't know what to say."

"Thanks, Sean," Joe responded. "I wish they *all* would come. I know I am not much to look at, but I sure need company. For so long I couldn't have company. Now I really want to see people and hear about their lives, even if it is how tough their teachers are. It will all be welcome news to me. It sure would break up the boredom and monotony."

Sean said, "Be careful about what you ask for. Report cards are coming out, and you might hear a lot of sad stories." That brought a smile to Joe's face, and a light chuckle rumbled out of his throat.

A nurse came in and said, "Joe, as much as I know you love company, that is enough for today. Tomorrow is a new day. You need to get some rest."

Charlene and Sean said goodbye to their friend and walked back down the hallway.

Charlene turned to Sean and asked, "How did you know?"

Sean said, "I saw his doctor at the drugstore. Joe was wanting and needing to see his friends. Doctors are just now inviting friends to come and visit Joe … but just don't overdo it."

Charlene said, "Tuesdays and Thursdays I will be here at the lab. I will drop in on him then. Maybe we can set up a schedule at school for people to visit him each day. What do you think?"

The two friends continued to make plans for hospital visitation as they made their way back to their vehicles.

Sean stopped and said, "Charlene, in two weeks there is a square dance. Will you go with me? I have asked for the night off."

Charlene looked at him and laughed. She shook her head and said, "You are one glutton for punishment. Your toenails haven't grown back from the damage I inflicted on your poor feet at the prom." They were laughing as they reached her car.

Sean said, "Let's go get a Coke and resume this conversation."

As they sat, sipping a cold drink, they discussed how to organize a hospital visitation chart. They agreed that in the morning they would approach the principal, requesting a chalkboard be set up for people to sign up to visit Joe. Maybe no more than two people at a time for each fifteen-minute block, limited to two hours each day. If that was too strenuous for Joe, then they would reduce the amount of time. And so, a plan was set in motion that would continue until Christmas break.

About a week after Charlene had sent James a letter, she received one in return.

Dear Charlene,

Again, this is a hard letter to write, but I must do it. I wasn't entirely honest with you. I had sort of broken up with my girlfriend. But since I have returned, we have gotten back together. She was Miss Rodeo at the last competition. She is really good looking, and she excites me. She is not much of a student, but she has other good qualities. I will not be writing to you anymore. This is it.

Goodbye, little next-door-neighbor girl.

James

Immediately Charlene wrote a return letter.

Dear James,

Thank you for letting me know. I will not bother you again.

Goodbye.

Charlene

Next, she wrote a letter to her daddy.

Dear Daddy,

It was exactly as you had guessed and warned me about with James. He has a girlfriend in Idaho. He was just sort of playing me along. Thank you for the warning. Mrs. Samuelson also warned me. Seems she had a feeling about him not being straight with me. Though it still hurts, it helped prepare me for the letter that came in today's mail.

Now to turn to a brighter and more pleasant subject, Sean and I are in the process of organizing a hospital visitation for students to visit Joe, the lone survivor of the tragic car accidents on prom night. We are trying to organize visits up until Christmas break.

Oh, speaking of Christmas break, Mother and Jerimiah are getting married around Christmas break. Good thing that the "dreams and wishes" trip to Idaho wasn't firmed up in light of everything I have told you in this letter. Jerimiah has bought a supercool house out in the country on some acreage. The house is up on a hill with a beautiful view of a valley below. I can't wait to see what that area looks like when leaves begin to change colors in the fall.

I must get to work on my homework.

Love you,
Charlene

At school the next day, after they had discussed plans for hospital visitation for Joe with the principal, Charlene asked Sean, "What do I wear to a square dance? Please help me. I have no idea as to what you have gotten me into."

He was quick with that smile and said, "That is easy. Do you have blue jeans and a checkered or western-style shirt? Cowboy boots would be optional. I suggest flat-heeled shoes. Put that hair up in a ponytail, and you are ready to go. Now wasn't that easy?"

"Yes," she replied, "easier than the dancing part."

Chapter 12

✦✦✦

After her lab work at the hospital, Charlene visited with Joe for a few minutes. When she walked through the door, his face lit up with a big smile.

He said, "Thank you for arranging for students to come visit me. You and Sean are the best. Say, did you say that James is Joyce's cousin? I didn't know they were related."

She nodded in the affirmative. "Yes, they are cousins. James had moved to Idaho before Joyce's family moved here for her dad to work on the dam. James used to be my next-door neighbor. That is why they were staying at our house. Joyce's folks had several people staying at their house, so James and his parents stayed with mother and me."

Joe said, "Now I understand why James didn't come to see me. We used to be pretty good friends in junior high. He was a cool guy, though he was a good student, and I wasn't. He was still a good friend."

He was silent for a minute or two, then said, "I understand that around Christmastime they are moving me to a rehab center. I will need to learn to walk again and to build my arm and leg muscles. They say I will be in rehab for about another year. Now that I am getting better, the school is looking at sending a visiting teacher to help me. The teacher will be bringing my assignments and will do one-on-one teaching. Hopefully, I will eventually graduate, but it will not be with you guys this school year."

Charlene replied, "I am glad the visiting teacher will be coming to help you catch up. Sean and I will need to find out when he or she will be here or at the rehab center in order that we don't have a bunch of kids come barging in to see you during class time."

Joe smiled and said, "I really wouldn't mind that, but I suspect that the teacher would." Then he laughed and asked, "Where will you and Sean plan on going to college? He wants to go into premed something or other. What about you?"

She replied, "We don't know yet. We have applied at some of the same colleges and universities. I plan to go into cancer research. He wants to study genetics. I suppose the two are related in some ways."

Joe shook his head. "You two are out of my league. I just hope to graduate. Period. I really wanted to go to a trade school, but now, who knows?"

Charlene said, "Joe, right now all you need to worry about is getting well and strong once more. You have a community pulling for you."

"Where is Sean? I expected him to come in with you," he replied.

She said, "On Tuesday and Thursdays I am doing labs here at the hospital. Sean is working at the drugstore. I clean Mrs. Samuelson's house on Mondays, Wednesdays, and Fridays. We each have a lot going on and then to keep up with homework, too. All of that keeps us both busy."

There was a knock on the door. Two more students dropped in for their scheduled time. Charlene said, "Hi, guys. He is all yours. Joe, see you next time. Keep up the good work." And she walked out the door as the two fellow students began their visit.

When Charlene arrived home, her mother had dinner just about ready to place on the table. They began chatting about their day and what all had gone on. Then Charlene asked about the wedding plans.

Margaret stopped what she was doing, took a deep breath, and shook her head. "I truly wonder why we just didn't elope. There is so much to arrange—flowers, cakes, the rehearsal dinner, guest lists, and on and on and on. My poor parents! May God rest their sweet souls. Now I understand what all they went through for my wedding to your father."

Jokingly Charlene said, "Does that mean when I am engaged, you won't mind if I elope?"

Margaret dropped her dish towel and said, "What did you just say? Are you engaged to James?"

Charlene sighed and said, "No, I am not engaged to James, nor anyone else. James has a Miss Rodeo he is in love with. He says she excites him. The letter I received from him was a Dear John letter. He is through with me. Better now than later."

Margaret said, "I bet his parents do not know this. They were excitedly hopeful that you two might get together. They will be disappointed. They are not very fond of her. They said she doesn't have a very good reputation. Oh well, I guess her good looks carry the weight with James. They were hoping things would cool off if he was away for a few days. But I guess not."

"I wrote him a note and told him that I wouldn't bother him again. I am done with him. I am focusing on schoolwork, my job, and my volunteer activities. When they left, I felt I would never see him again. I refuse to look back over my shoulder at what might have been. Those were simply dreams and wishes.

"On to a much happier note. Sean invited me to go with him to a square dance. I need a checkered or western-style shirt and blue jeans. I told him he is a glutton for punishment. He is a good sport and such a good friend. He makes me laugh a lot."

Margaret said, "Tomorrow after you go to Mrs. Samuelson's house, drop by the store and buy jeans and a shirt. Get anything else you might need, like a neckerchief or something for your hair. Believe me, Sean will be happy with the way you look, but his toes may do some complaining about your dancing." And they both burst into laughter.

When Charlene knocked on Mrs. Samuelson's door, she heard, "The door is not locked. Come on in."

Charlene thought that was very strange—not at all like her usual greeting. When she entered the door, she saw Mrs. Samuelson lying on the floor.

She said, "Child, I knew you would be here on time. I am so glad you are here. Please help me. Can you reach the phone for me? Call my daughter. Tell her that I have fallen."

Charlene picked up the phone and dialed the number. When Mrs. Jacobson came on the phone, Charlene told her that her mother had fallen and needed help.

Her daughter said, "I'm calling an ambulance right now. Stay with her."

Charlene said, "I will be right here. I am not going anywhere."

When they hung up, Charlene grabbed some pillows off the sofa and placed them under Mrs. Samuelson's head; then she covered her with an afghan. She sat on the floor beside Mrs. Samuelson and held her hand. She asked her how long she had been on the floor. Mrs. Samuelson thought she had been there about half an hour.

Charlene asked her whether she was in pain.

The response? "Oh! Mercy yes, child, my hip is hurting terribly. Are you sure the ambulance is coming?"

Charlene assured her help should be arriving any minute. She kept Mrs. Samuelson talking and asked whether there was anything she could do to make her more comfortable.

The answer with force was "Just get that ambulance here!" Charlene kept telling her they were coming.

Loud footsteps came up the steps and crossed the wooden porch floor. Charlene dashed to the door and threw it open. They were the EMTs, and were bringing a gurney.

They asked Charlene to stand to one side, saying, "We have it now."

Charlene said, "Oh, please be careful with her. She said her hip is really hurting!"

One of the three EMTs said, "Thank you for telling us that. We will get her to the hospital as quickly as we can."

About that time, Mrs. Jacobson came dashing in the front door. She saw Charlene and asked, "Where is she?"

Charlene pointed and said, "She said she fell about a half hour ago. Her hip is hurting terribly. When I knocked on the door, she called out for me to come in. The door wasn't locked. That is where I found her."

The EMTs had placed a backboard under Mrs. Samuelson and were gently positioning her on the gurney. They soon had her loaded into the ambulance; with the siren sounding, they sped down the street.

Mrs. Jacobson told Charlene there was no need for her to stay. She was free to go for the day.

Mrs. Jacobson locked the door, and as the two women walked down the sidewalk to their cars, Sean came speeding up in his reliable, old, beat-up pickup.

He hopped out of his truck and asked, "What happened?"

They explained about Mrs. Samuelson's fall.

Mrs. Jacobson asked Sean how he knew the ambulance had been coming here.

He said, "We have a police scanner in the drugstore, and I heard she had fallen. I came to see if I could be of help."

Mrs. Jacobson said, "No, there is nothing to do at the moment. Thank you for coming. I need to get to the hospital and start filling out paper work. Thank you, Charlene, for being here today. Mother has said so many times how she knows she can depend on you."

Charlene said, "We will be praying for her. Do you want me to wait with you at the hospital?"

Mrs. Jacobson said, "No, that will not be necessary. My husband should be at the ER by the time I get there. Thanks again." With that she got in her car and sped away.

After she left, Charlene started to cry. She said, "Mrs. Samuelson was in so much pain, and I could do nothing. I felt so helpless."

Sean put his arms around her and held her tightly against him as she cried. Sean said, "It is going to be all right. You were here for her. You got her help. You helped her. It is going to be okay."

By now neighbors had gathered, wanting to know what had happened. Charlene explained about finding Mr. Samuelson lying on the floor where she had fallen, adding that her daughter had been here and that they were at the hospital right now. Continuing,

Charlene said, "Thank you for coming to check on her. She was complaining of her hip hurting. She is in the ER."

Charlene realized Sean was still holding her in his arms. Strange that he had been the one to be there when she needed him.

Sean said, "Let's go get a Coke, okay?" He opened her car door for her to get in. She was still wiping tears from her face when he leaned down and kissed her. Then he gave her one of those priceless smiles.

He said, "See you in a couple of minutes."

This time, instead of being seated at a table, they sat in a booth side by side. He slid his arm over her shoulders and sat very close to her.

Charlene whispered to him, "Thank you for coming to check on things at Mrs. Samuelson's house."

He tenderly reached up, brushed a tear from her cheek, and said, "I am glad I could be there."

After they had finished their cold drinks, Sean said, "Do you want to drop by the hospital to see how she is doing? We can also look in on Joe. You can leave your car here and ride with me."

When they located Mrs. Jacobson and family, the waiting area was filled with concerned friends and family. They were told that she was in surgery and that they should be getting an update on her progress very soon. They were introduced to Mrs. Samuelson's grandchildren and various neighbors and friends.

One neighbor said, "Oh, you are the young lady who found her. It is nice to meet you."

The two-young people waited until a medical doctor came out to say, "She is out of surgery and doing well."

From around the room of people, there was a chorus of "Praise the Lord!"

Charlene and Sean told Mrs. Jacobson they would check on her tomorrow, and they exited the waiting area.

They went down the hall to see Joe. He was happy to see them. He said, "Say, look at the two of you. You're getting to be an item.

Glad to see this happening. Why are you here now? This isn't your scheduled time, or do I have my schedule mixed up?"

They explained about Mrs. Samuelson's fall and the surgery. They said they'd decided to drop in and check on him to make sure he wasn't giving the nurses any trouble.

About that time a voice said, "What's this about giving the nurses trouble?"

They looked around, and there was Dr. Hayden. He said, "What are you kids doing? Trying to keep our unruly patient in line? Believe me, it is a full-time job. He is getting full of himself now that he is having so much company. He is doing so much better that he seems to be trying to get himself kicked out of the hospital. He must not like our room service. Oh well, it looks like he is going to succeed at getting kicked out of here sometime in the near future. We plan to move him to the rehab center within the next few days—that is, if no surprises pop up."

Then, as if for the first time, he saw Joe and continued, "Oh, hello, Joe. What is going on today? Don't tell me that these two are more of your friends!" And he continued joking with Joe and soon had Joe laughing and in good spirits.

Chuckling to themselves, Charlene and Sean left Joe in Dr. Hayden's capable hands. Sean caught Charlene's hand as they walked along.

He said, "Charlene, you have no idea how much I care for you." Before he could say anymore, they met another group of students on their way to visit Joe.

Charlene said, "Shouldn't you be at work? Your boss will think you have run away."

Sean responded with a big smile. "I would be happy for that to happen if I could run away with you."

Charlene playfully pushed him on the shoulder and laughed, saying, "In the meantime there is work to be done. Take me to the 'little blue machine.'"

The following day, after Charlene had completed two hours in the lab, she visited with Mrs. Samuelson. She was pleasantly surprised to see Mrs. Samuelson seated in a chair. Her hip had been a clean break; consequently, a few pins and screws stabilized the broken bones. She was fortunate that she didn't have to do the big hip surgery.

Charlene learned that Mrs. Samuelson had tripped on a small rug in the hallway. She said again how happy she had been when she heard Charlene's footsteps on the steps and then on the porch.

Charlene said, "I think a mysterious person should enter your house and 'steal' all of those throw rugs before they throw you again!" That brought the nod of a head and a chuckle from Mrs. Samuelson.

The two friends talked for some time. Eventually, she asked Charlene about James.

Charlene told her he had sent her a Dear John letter.

It was at that time that Mrs. Samuelson said, "Charlene, I am a pretty good judge of character. That young man wouldn't meet my eyes. He hardly spoke to me. He was anxious to be on his way. I didn't trust him. When I said, 'I am glad you brought him out to meet me,' I sincerely meant it. However, I didn't trust him. I wasn't sure how to tell you without offending you. Sweet child, there are a lot of fish in the ocean. Don't just settle for just anyone. I was thrilled when you went to the prom with Sean. Now that young man is solid. If you haven't already done so, I suggest that you take another good look or three or four at him. He is a good guy."

Charlene laughed. "Thank you for those comments. I received *the* letter from James several days ago, and about Sean, we will be going to a square dance. Poor guy! I told my mother that his poor toenails hadn't healed from the damage I did to him at the prom, and here he is, asking me out again."

Mrs. Samuelson's nurse came in and said, "I think you need to get back in bed. You have been in that chair for quite a while. Sorry, Charlene, but I am taking her away from you."

Charlene leaned over, gave Mrs. Samuelson a gentle hug, and told her goodbye, with a promise to see her again in a day or two.

From there she went a few doors down from Mrs. Samuelson's room to see Joe.

When she walked into Joe's room, he was angrily yelling at one of the nurses. When he saw Charlene, he shouted, even louder, "I am sick and tired of being in this hospital and unable to do anything for myself. You have no idea how depressing this can be!"

Charlene said, "That is a true statement. I have no idea how sick of being in here you must be. But rest assured, they will not keep you one second more than they have to. Please work with them to help get you better so you can be released. And please be nice to these angels of mercy. They want you well just about as badly—or maybe even more so—than you want to be well. Anyway, anyone who can fuss and complain as much as I just heard you doing has to be a lot better than when you came into this hospital."

Joe stopped, looked at her, and chuckled. He looked at the nurse and said, "I am sorry that I was yelled at you. And Charlene, you did it again. You put me in my place *again*. That wasn't the first time you have done that. The other time made a deep impression on me. My guess is, you just gave me something else to think about when I am lying awake at night."

The nurse walked past Charlene, patted her on the shoulder, and said, "Thanks for intervening. I owe you one." She exited through the door.

Charlene said, "I have just a few minutes to visit with you. I just wanted to see how you are doing. I need to get home and take care of a writing assignment and some other things. Christmas break is coming fast. My mother's wedding is approaching, and a square dance is this weekend. I have a lot to finish before we break for the holidays."

Joe said, "Are you going to the dance with Sean? He is one lucky dog. I never thought I would say this, but I wish I was in school, working on homework. I have learned so much through this accident, lessons I never wanted to learn."

Charlene replied, "My guess is, you are truly feeling that way right now. You can't go back and undo things, but you can make things different in the future. You promised me the first time I visited you after the accident that, after you got out of the hospital, you would visit middle schools and high schools and tell them what happened on prom night. I am holding you to that promise. You promised me that you would warn other students. Please don't break that promise."

"Charlene, you are tough on a guy. All right, I will keep my promise to you."

Quickly she glanced at her watch and said, "Joe, I need to go. I will drop in soon. Take care."

He said, "Aren't you going to tell me no more yelling at nurses?"

She replied, "I leave that decision up to you. You know what is right. Bye." With that, she left the room.

At the nurses' station, Charlene spoke to them and asked, "How much longer will he be here before he is moved to rehab?"

One of the nurses said, "As soon as we can get the infection cleaned up in his leg. He still has a long way to go."

Dr. Hayden walked into the station and said, "I think we need to put you on the payroll. You 'tamed the tiger' better than anyone on our team. You have a gift, Charlene."

She smiled and said, "He certainly seemed to be in a bad humor tonight when I came in. Bye, everyone. I'll see you next time."

As she walked away from the nurse's station, Dr. Hayden said, "What an amazing young woman. God certainly has something great planned for her."

Chapter 13

◆◆◆

The square dance was fast approaching in three days. Charlene dropped by the drugstore to see Sean after her lab time was completed. They visited for a few minutes before a customer entered the building.

As she was leaving, she said, "I just dropped by to tell you that you have a few days left to back out and save your toes before the dance."

The customer overheard what she had said and said, "Sean, here is a nice footbath I can recommend in case your dance partner is a little rough on you."

They were all laughing.

Sean replied, "Thanks for the recommendation. I will remember that just in case she has to give me a foot massage."

Laughing, Charlene shook her head, waved at them, and walked out the door.

Margaret was all in a twitter when Charlene walked in the door. The wedding was about three weeks away. She told Charlene that flowers and cakes were ordered, the rehearsal dinner was planned, the church was reserved, the dress was bought, and Charlene's dress and shoes were ordered. Invitations had been sent out. Few RSVPs had been returned.

Margaret said, "It makes it very hard to plan when people do not respond and let us know who is or is not coming to the wedding. I am all flustered over it."

Mother and daughter discussed the wedding, the move to the big house, and what to do with their home—the only home Charlene had ever known. They agreed and marveled that anything so beautiful and meaningful as a wedding could be so stressful.

After dinner, Charlene went to her room and began her nightly ritual of homework. But first she wrote her daddy a letter. She told him about Mrs. Samuelson's accident, Joe's cantankerous behavior, and the upcoming square dance. Last of all, she mentioned Margaret's approaching wedding.

In this letter, there was no mention of James; nor would there be any mention of him in future correspondence. However, more and more was said about Sean. Sean was someone she could depend on. She painted a picture of a very remarkable young man.

Jerimiah came over Saturday morning to move some of Margaret's packed boxes to the new house. He had asked Sean to come along and give him a hand. Charlene went with the two men to the new house to deliver the boxes. The house was beginning to look beautiful with new furniture in place.

Charlene walked around inside, admiring the new house. She thought, *I have never lived anywhere except for our little house in town. I don't see that I can ever feel like this lovely place is my home. But then I will only be here for about six months.*

Then she walked outside and was standing there, overlooking the valley far below and just daydreaming, when Sean came up and slipped his arms around her waist. He rested his chin on her head and said, "Remember when we came here after Sunday dinner with Jerimiah and your mother? I was standing here, looking at the valley, when you asked me, 'What?' I responded, 'Oh, nothing.' Well, there was something on my mind. I wanted so badly to buy you a place like this for us to have one day. Charlene, I think I am in love with you."

She turned around in his arms, stood on her tiptoes, and slipped her arms around his neck. She gave him a kiss and said, "I would love that too. Maybe someday."

He responded, "If we get scholarships to the same school, will you marry me before we go off to college? That way we can help each other with our studies. Please say yes. I know it will be hard, but we can do it. Neither of us is used to living high. We can make it work. We may eat a lot of ramen noodles. We can share household duties, study together, and be together forever."

Charlene said, "If we can get into the same college, then yes, I will marry you. You are my rock. I love you."

Before the conversation could continue, Jerimiah came walking across the yard and said, "It is about time for us to load up and head back into town to see if there is something else we can help your mother with."

Hand in hand Charlene and Sean walked back to Jerimiah's pickup. Their hearts pounded with excitement because of an unfinished conversation.

The moving from house to house had begun. It would be a bittersweet moment. Happiness for her mother and sadness to give up her little home.

Saturday night soon arrived. Sean came to take her to the square dance. She was dressed in well-fitting blue jeans and a western-style shirt with a bright-colored handkerchief tied around her neck. Her hair had been drawn up high in a perky ponytail. She had the right amount of makeup on, and as her mother said, she was as "cute as a bug!" Whatever that meant.

Sean led her to a beginners' group, and Charlene was introduced to square dancing. It wasn't long until she caught on to the commands the square dance caller was saying, and soon she fell in step. Sean told her she had good rhythm and was catching on quickly.

Some of the girls and women had on very full, circular skirts with layers and layers of fluffy, net crinolines petticoats underneath. The old-timers had matching outfits for couples. She watched them and could tell they had been dance partners for many, many years.

After the evening was over, Charlene said, "I feel like I have been to first day of gym class. That is a lot of work! The experienced dancers make it look so easy. Thank you for introducing me to something else in your world."

When Sean walked her to the front door, he held her in his arms and kissed her. He said, "Charlene, I am crazy about you. I hate being away from you for even one second. I have to admit I want to be with you forever." With that he kissed her once again.

She held him tightly and responded, "I think you are pretty fantastic, too. Thank you for a fun evening. I better go into the house now. Will I see you at church tomorrow?"

The next weeks flew by. Margaret and Jerimiah were married. The family moved into the new home. Mrs. Samuelson was released from the hospital and was resting at home. Charlene continued to be with her and do housework for two hours on Mondays, Wednesdays, and Fridays. Charlene's lab work continued, along with visits with Joe, who had moved to a rehab facility.

At the lab, one of the techs showed Charlene a smear on a slide of the infection that had come from Joe's leg. Identifying the type of infection helped the doctors to prescribe the correct treatment to clear it up.

The Christmas holidays happened in all the mix and were very nice nonetheless. And now the last half of their senior year of high school had arrived.

Correspondence arrived from various colleges and universities. Sean and Charlene spent many hours comparing which schools would serve their educational needs to their greatest advantage. Each time an envelope arrived with new information, the two hopeful students eagerly ripped it open to see what opportunities for scholarships might be waiting inside.

Sean and Charlene went on a date as often as their two busy schedules permitted. Feelings for one another grew deeper by the day.

Chapter 14

◆◆◆

The end of the school year drew down to days. The school counselor continued to work steadily with Sean and Charlene on college placement. Colleges and universities Sean and Charlene had contacted were asking for their transcripts.

One morning the school counselor sent a message for the two of them to come to her office. She said, "I understand you two sent letters of inquiry to Johns Hopkins University. They requested your transcripts and are very interested in the two of you. I understand they seldom choose two students from the same school. They are very impressed with your interest in the medical field. They have received letters of recommendations from several of the doctors and medical people in our local hospital plus several residents of Wilsonville. Plus, they are very interested in your grade point averages. They are offering you each a four-year scholarship so long as you maintain your GPA. Congratulations to the both of you."

Immediately the two speechless students looked at each other and gave each other a big hug. They had to be careful on school grounds, there would be "no public display of affection," better known as PDA. They gave each other a very long and knowing look, each knowing the other's thoughts.

Charlene found her voice and said, "Thank you. I don't know what to say, but thank you." Happy tears streamed down her face.

Sean also thanked the counselor. Then Principal Taylor came into the office, along with Pastor Jones, Mr. and Mrs. Stevenson, Jerimiah, and Margaret, to shake their hands, give hugs, and congratulate them on their well-earned accomplishments. This was a day these two young adults would long remember.

The rest of the school day was simply a blur. Charlene was anxious to tell Mrs. Samuelson and Dr. Hayden the news.

In class Sean whispered to her, "This is Friday, and I am asking off from work tonight. I will call you. I have something I want to give you."

Charlene couldn't wait to get to Mrs. Samuelson's house. She wanted to see her face when she told her the good news.

True to her form, Mrs. Samuelson was as excited as Charlene. The two chatted and laughed, and the house was filled with excitement once again. Charlene quickly turned to her chores, humming a happy tune and whizzing around while dusting, polishing, and shining the house.

Sean called while she was at Mrs. Samuelson's house. He would pick her up around eight o'clock, and they would go out for dinner. He said, "Wear something sort of like, you know, like you wear to church."

Mrs. Samuelson smiled as big as could be. She was delighted that these two-young people she was so fond of were going out on a date.

Charlene dashed home. She thought, *still feels odd not to be going to my little home that I had lived in all my life but to the beautiful home on a hill.* She hadn't been home very long when Margaret arrived. Jerimiah would be later due to a case in court lasting longer than he had planned. She explained to her mother that Sean was taking her out to dinner at eight o'clock.

She said, "He said that he has something he wants to give me. Oh, Mother, today has been so amazing. I am having trouble believing this is all actually happening. Can you believe it? Premed? Johns Hopkins? And going there with Sean. I am so excited. Sean is so wonderful. Don't you think so? Oh, listen to me chatter. I just can't contain myself."

Margaret just smiled and said, "Honey, I am so proud of you. You have earned every good thing that is coming your way. And yes, Sean is wonderful. He is all I have heard this school year, well, with one minor interruption. Yes, I think he is wonderful. Here is a letter for you from your dad. Don't you think you need to grab a quick shower and start getting ready for your date? Why don't you wear that white, sleeveless dress? It looks very nice on you. And you have those new sandals. You will be as cute as a bug."

Charlene took the letter from her mother's hand. She opened it and began reading.

> Dear Charlene,
>
> The end of school will be here in one week. I plan to be there for your graduation. Have you found out anything about the scholarships? Wherever you attend, I want to send you an allowance each month to help with your other expenses. Sorry I can't pay for your whole education, but I want to do what I can. Let me know the time of graduation and what you have heard about colleges.
>
> I love you,
> Dad

Charlene quickly grabbed a sheet of paper and dashed off a letter.

> Dear Daddy,
>
> Funny you should ask. Your letter arrived today, and today I learned that Sean and I have received four-year premed scholarships to Johns Hopkins University. The school counselor called Sean and me out of class to come to her office. We went to see what she wanted. That is when we learned about our scholarships. She had called Mother and Jerimiah, Mr. and Mrs. Stevenson, Pastor Jones, and the principal to tell all of us the good news.

Sean and I have been inseparable this school year, except for one almost interruption. We have developed a very deep and intense relationship. It seems he is always there when I need him. He is so reliable. I really think the world of him.

Speaking of Sean, I have a date with him at eight o'clock tonight. He said he has something to give me. I better get ready. I am looking forward to seeing you at my graduation next Friday night at seven o'clock at the high school auditorium. Don't forget!

Love you,
Charlene

Dressed and ready, Charlene was seated at the bay window, waiting for Sean, when she saw his pickup coming up the driveway. She called to her mother, "Sean is here. I'll see you later. Thank Jerimiah for coming to school today. I'll thank him again myself when I see him. He is really a nice guy. Tell him that his coming really meant a lot to me. Love you."

Sean was standing at the door, looking as handsome as ever, with that big smile on his face, as if he knew something the world didn't know anything about.

When she exited the door, he put his arms around her and gave her a kiss.

He said, "You really look great! I like that dress. Have I seen that one?"

She caught his arm, put her face against him, and said, "No, you haven't seen it. It is new. Jerimiah is so good to me. He is acting like a doting father. I was so happy he came to school today. Wasn't today amazing?"

By now they had reached the pickup. He opened her door and helped her in, then reached over, gave her a big kiss, and said, "I hope tonight will be just as memorable."

Charlene watched him as he walked around to the driver's side of the pickup. She said, "Well, my handsome Mr. Mystery Man, what do you have up your sleeve?"

He grinned that million-dollar smile and said, "At the right time and the right moment, you will find out."

By now they were driving down the curvy driveway, each chattering away about the news of the day.

Charlene said, "I had a letter from my dad today, and he said he will send me an allowance each month while I am in college and that he hoped it would help with other expenses. Right now, along with making my car and insurance payments, he sends me gas money each month. He wants to know where I, rather we, will be going to college and what time graduation is scheduled. He plans to be here for that.

"Oh! Listen to me talk! I have not given you a chance to say anything. What has gone on in your life since I saw you this afternoon?"

He said, "Take off your seat belt, put on the center seat belt, slide over, and sit by me. This old truck has a center seat belt you can use. You are too far away over there."

"Well, I talked with my parents about us. Seems that is all I ever talk about—you and me. I have told them everything about you, even what you said at prom night when the group was going to the next town to spend the night. I told them that you said, 'I am saving myself for my husband on my wedding night, and I sure don't want to go throw everything away like that!' They both said, 'She really said that in a group? She is amazing. You better watch her that some other guy doesn't snatch her away from you. She is worth holding on to.' And Charlene, I want to hold on to you for the rest of our lives."

She leaned her head on his shoulder and said, "Sean, your parents actually said that about me?"

He said, "Yes. My mother is a member of the same club Mrs. Samuelson is in. You are the topic of conversation. Charlene, you have no idea how well loved you are by this town. You have shown the town that just because you are dirt poor doesn't mean you can't succeed if you are willing to work your butt off. Oops, sorry, but you know what I mean."

Charlene said, "That is so sweet! By the way, where are we going? We are not going back to take another night class, are we?"

Sean laughed and said, "No, I promise you, no night classes."

Soon they were pulling into the parking lot of a nice restaurant.

Big-eyed Charlene said, "Sean, you shouldn't be spending your hard-earned money like this. You need to save it for college!"

While she was talking, his lips met hers and silenced her protest. Then he said, "My dad gave me the money for tonight. Come on. I am starved."

He caught her hand and helped her out of the pickup. She turned, looked at the pickup, and said, "I just love that pickup!" He smiled all the more. Hand in hand, they approached the entry way to a nice restaurant.

After a delicious meal had been consumed, they were savoring the day and evening and enjoying one another's company when Sean reached into his pocket and pulled out a small box. He sat it in front of her and said, "Open it." Slowly her hands touched the velvet-covered box and opened it. Inside was a gorgeous ring.

Sean said, "Charlene, the other day I meant it when I said, 'If we can get scholarships at the same school, I want to marry you.' Well, we have the scholarships. Now, will you marry me? This was my grandmother's ring. My parents said if it needs to be resized, they will take it to a jewelry store and have it taken care of. Will you be my bride?" He took the ring from the box and slipped it on her finger. The ring fit perfectly. He said "Charlene, say something. I've known you for almost thirteen years, and I have never seen you speechless."

With misty eyes, she looked into his adoring face and said, "I would love to be your bride. Are you sure you trust me with something as precious and beautiful as your grandmother's ring? Just look at it!"

Sliding his plate to one side, he reached across the table, pulled her toward him, and kissed her. Smiling broadly, the manager walked over to their table. Looking up at him, Sean said, "We just became engaged to be married. Look at her ring. It was my grandmother's."

The manager said, "Congratulations. Tonight's meal is on the house. And may you have a long and happy life together. Are you two out of high school?"

Sean spoke up and said, "We graduate this coming Friday. We will be attending Johns Hopkins University this fall. Today we learned we each will have a four-year premed scholarship. Today has been a banner day. I wanted to bring her here to your restaurant tonight to celebrate and to become engaged."

The manager asked, "What do you two plan to do with your lives?"

Sean turned to Charlene and said, "You want to answer that?"

She said, "Sure. Sean plans to eventually do genetic research, and I plan to become a cancer research scientist. We had planned and hoped that we could attend the same college and had planned, if it worked out that way, that we would be married before we leave for school. Now we are hoping to be married before we move out east this fall."

The manager had pulled up a chair and sat down. "Never have I had the privilege of talking to two high school kids who have such concrete plans. Where do you live?"

Sean replied, "We live in Wilsonville."

The manager said, "That is not far away, only about a twenty-minute drive. Here is my card. I would love to do the rehearsal dinner for your wedding, if your parents do not have other plans. How large of a group are you planning?"

Sean laughed and said, "Whoa! We don't know all that yet. I suspect the rehearsal dinner will be rather small. The wedding will be larger, of course. We probably won't have a large wedding party. We are a couple of poor kids whose families were impacted by the factory closing some four years ago. We have had to scrape and dig for everything we have."

The manager, undeterred, continued. "For two kids who have come so far, I want to be a part of your wedding. I will make your parents a very special deal on the rehearsal dinner, contact me and let me know the date. I'll see what I can do for you, if your parents do not have other plans. These little rural towns don't often have students who have achieved what you two have done. You will represent our town, too. What are your names?"

"I am Sean Stevenson, and this is my fiancée, Charlene Jamison. You can call Wilsonville High School and speak with the school counselor to verify our story. You are welcome to do that."

The manager said, "Nice meeting you two. I am Tom Jackson, the manager. I am sure I will be reading about the two of you in the paper. Small-town papers like to brag about their students. Say, didn't Wilsonville have a tragic car accident with several students dying several months back?"

Sean said, "Yes, sir. They would have been in our senior class. There were six students involved. Five died, and there is one lone survivor still in a convalescent center. He will be there about another year. He is having to learn to walk all over again. Our town has been hard hit the past few years."

The manager shook his head and had a sad expression on his face. Then he said, "But now we have you two to celebrate and bring new hope to the community. Thanks for coming to my restaurant tonight. Someday you can tell your grandchildren about tonight. Good luck in your futures as you battle cancer and genetic defects. God bless you both. Come again. Be sure to tell your parents what I have offered you. Congratulations on your engagement and everything. Good night and drive safely."

The happy couple drove to Sean's home. Charlene had never been to his house. His parents were waiting for them. When Sean and Carlene walked into the front door, Mr. and Mrs. Stevenson rushed to them, exclaiming on how happy they were that they had stopped by.

Charlene showed them her ring and said, "Are you sure you want me to have something as precious as this ring, which belonged to your parent? Don't you want to keep it for yourself? It is so lovely!"

Mr. Stevenson said, "That was my mother's ring. She said she wanted Sean to give it to his bride someday. And Sean has told us all about you and said he wants to marry you. I am taking it that he received a yes answer since you are wearing that ring." They gave her a big hug and said, "Welcome to our family."

Sean stood to one side, smiling like there was no tomorrow.

Mrs. Stevenson said, "We don't want to keep you from going on over to tell your folks the good news. We are so proud of you both. Here, I need another hug."

With that the two left for the drive up the hill to tell Margaret and Jerimiah.

When they pulled into the driveway, the porch lights were turned on, and Margaret and Jerimiah were in the living room.

When they walked into the room, Charlene said, "Mother, look!" Sean held out her hand, displaying the beautiful ring. "We are engaged and plan to marry before we leave for college. Good thing you and Jerimiah have the experience of how to do things, because now you can say, 'Here we go again!' I am so excited I could pop!"

Jerimiah was already shaking Sean's hand, patting him on his back, and congratulating him.

Margaret said, "Really? Are you serious? You're not joking, are you?"

Charlene said, "Those words sound remarkably like what I said to you and Jerimiah a few months back. No, we aren't joking. We had discussed that if we should get accepted to the same college with scholarships that we would be married. Well, here it is!"

Jerimiah said, "Come over here and sit down. Tell us everything. Your mother is in shock. You are her baby. But she will recover."

Sean told them about going to the restaurant; there Tom Jackson, the manager, had visited with them. "He was very interested in our plans for the future and about our engagement. He even gave me cards to give to our parents, saying he would give you guys a great deal on a rehearsal dinner. Here is yours, Jerimiah. I have one for my parents."

Jerimiah took the card and said, "I know Tom. He is a good man. I am glad you went to his restaurant."

Sean said, "He even said that since we were engaged at his restaurant tonight, the meal was on the house. Did you see Charlene's ring? It belonged to my grandmother, my daddy's mother. She had said that she wanted me to give it to my bride someday, and now I have." He smiled with pride.

Margaret said, "Sean, it is a lovely ring. How can I be happy and sad at the same time? Sean, you are a wonderful guy, and I am so happy you and Charlene are engaged, but like Jerimiah says, *she is my baby.*"

Charlene said, "We want to be married before we go out east to school. Will it put too much pressure on you two? We do not want a large wedding party, but the reception may be a different story. You both have friends and relatives, and all our school friends and teachers, doctors, and medical people will want to attend the wedding. I'm not sure where we can hold the wedding. Mr. Tom Jackson said we are bringing hope back to the town. The town does need something to celebrate. I wish it wasn't so late. I would go tell Mrs. Samuelson. But I will do that tomorrow. Sean, my head is spinning!" They were all laughing at her disjointed, happy chatter.

Margaret said, "Sean, why don't you call your parents and ask them to come over. I will make a pot of coffee. Good thing I made a cake today."

Immediately he jumped up and called his mom and dad. He said, "They will be here shortly. We stopped by the house to tell them when we came into town. Charlene showed them her ring, and they saw that it fit perfectly. My parents had said that if it didn't, they would take it to a jewelry store and have it sized to fit her finger. But it fits." He and Charlene were seated on the sofa as close as possible. When he was talking about her ring, he admired the ring on the hand of his prospective bride.

A few minutes later, Mr. and Mrs. Stevenson were at the door. Happy greetings were exchanged, and they were invited in to join the celebration.

Jerimiah said, "Sean, it looks like your mother and Margaret need to get together and get the ball rolling. Just thinking out loud, I truly think our church will not be large enough to hold this wedding. You know the community will want to come together for this celebration.

It has been a long time since something has happened that the whole town can celebrate. I think Tom was exactly right on that. What do you think about City Park? The ceremony could be in the gazebo. Like I said, I am just thinking out loud. If you like the idea, I can talk with the city council, or whoever it is, about reserving the park for your special day. I don't know if it is appropriate for a stepfather to be so excited or involved in a wedding of his stepdaughter. But I *am* excited and want to be involved. I love you, Charlene, as much as if you were my own flesh and blood. I guess I am like Charlene. I am chatting away like crazy."

The others chimed in, saying, "We like your idea."

Charlene went to Jerimiah, hugged him, and said, "And yes, you do have every right to be involved. I like your idea too. And I love you. Thank you for all the things you have done for Mother and me." She returned to her place at Sean's side.

Mrs. Stevenson said, "Jerimiah, please call us Nell and Richard. We have known Margaret for many years. Our kids have grown up together. Anyway, now that that is out of the way, we will just have to pray for good weather. If not, where would a backup place be for the event? The high school gym? Oh well, that will all work out."

The last item discussed was a date. What date would be possible? How to match schedules? A tentative date was set for August first. Size of the wedding party? Sean and Charlene said, "Small."

Charlene asked, "Could I have Mrs. Samuelson as my matron of honor? I could ask Mary Sue James to be my maid of honor. We have been friends since kindergarten. What do you think?

Sean said, "I would like to ask Joe to be one of my groomsmen and Charlie Samson. A ramp would have to be installed to get Joe's wheelchair into the gazebo. What do you think?"

From there other items of discussion followed: invitations, Tom's offer for the rehearsal dinner to be held at his restaurant, colors, flowers, cakes, punch, and so forth. And so, the conversation went on until well after midnight. The two families were now one in the purpose of having a nice wedding for their children.

Finally, Mrs. Stevenson said, "Look at the clock. Our children have kept us out way past our curfew. We better call it a night. Maybe we can go out to lunch after church on Sunday. Oh, that reminds me. We better ask the pastor if he will do the honor of officiating at the wedding. Let's go home before we find something else to talk about."

With that everyone stood to his or her feet and headed to the door. There were hugs and congratulations voiced as well as "Good night, all."

Charlene walked Sean to his pickup. He held her tightly, and they gave each other a long kiss. Charlene stepped back and said, "Good night, Sean. I love you."

Sean grabbed one more kiss and reluctantly slipped into his pickup. He turned and, with that dynamite smile, said, "Good night, future Mrs. Stevenson."

And so, ended an incredible day.

Chapter 15

❖❖❖

Saturday morning was a beautiful, sunshiny day; birds were singing, and Charlene was buzzing around, doing weekend chores, when she turned to Margaret and said, "As soon as I finish my chores, I want to go into town, show Mrs. Samuelson my ring, and ask her whether she will be my matron of honor. Then I want to go to the lab at the hospital. I am so happy. I am about to explode."

Margaret said, "Go on now! Your head is in the clouds. Go and share your good news with your friends."

With that Charlene dashed out of the house and into her little blue car. First stop was Mrs. Samuelson.

When she rang the doorbell, Mrs. Samuelson came to the door and was surprised to see Charlene. She said, "What a surprise! Child, what are you doing here today?"

Charlene stuck out her left hand and said, "Sean and I are engaged. We have dated most of the school year but have known each other since we were five. Oh, Mrs. Samuelson, Sean and I have each received four-year scholarships to Johns Hopkins University. We are going to be married before we leave for the East Coast. Mrs. Samuelson, will you be my matron of honor?"

Chuckling merrily, Mrs. Samuelson led her by the hand into the house. All the while, Charlene chatted like a magpie. They were soon seated at the round table where they had enjoyed so many conversations. Mrs. Samuelson said, "Tell me every detail and don't leave out one tiny thing. Oh yes, Sean is a wonderful young man. He reminds me of my own precious husband. Oh, this is so romantic. Of course, I will be happy to be your matron of honor. But who ever heard of a grandmother being a matron of honor. Well, they will now!" And she chuckled some more.

Soon Charlene said, "I need to go to the lab at the hospital and tell them about our premed scholarships and our engagement—that is, if Sean has not already done so." She gave Mrs. Samuelson a big hug and a kiss on her cheek. Then she dashed out the door. Mrs. Samuelson waved at her from the porch as she drove away.

Mrs. Samuelson said, "There is nothing like young love."

Charlene pulled into the hospital parking lot, and as she was approaching the large columns at the front doors, Sean came out. At the same time, both said, "What are you doing here?" Then they laughed and hugged each other.

Sean had been to see Joe, and the nurse had come in the room when he was telling Joe about the engagement. Soon the other nurses came in to congratulate him. And then Dr. Hayden said, "What is this I hear? My best volunteer is going to marry you? You are stealing her away from us." He laughed and shook Sean's hand, patting him on the back.

Joe said, "He is one lucky dog!"

Charlene said, "Well, come with me. I'm going into the lab to tell them. I want them to meet you."

When they walked through the doors into the lab, the supervisor looked up and saw Charlene and Sean. She said, "What are you doing here today? This is Saturday. I dropped in about a case and here you are."

Charlene said, "Everyone, this is Sean. We have some news we want to tell everyone." She stuck out her hand so they could see her beautiful ring. She said, "We are engaged to be married. And get this—we both have four-year scholarships to Johns Hopkins University. I just had to come in today and tell everyone. Thank you, all, for helping me with my extra-credit work in this lab. So much has happened in the past twenty-four hours that I am about to pop."

The lab techs had pulled off their gloves and goggles and congratulated Sean and Charlene.

One of them said, "Does Dr. Hayden know about this? If not, you better scramble down the hall and see him. You can't leave him out of this."

Sean and Charlene waved bye to everyone and went on down the hallway. Soon they found Dr. Hayden.

He came over and said to Charlene, "What is this you have done? You are going to leave us for this tall drink of water? He better be good to you, or I will come out east and bring you back home." He hugged her and congratulated Sean once more.

Charlene said, "Did Sean tell you that we each have received a four-year scholarship to Johns Hopkins University? We plan to be married before we leave for the East Coast. We had to come to tell everyone today. I think we may as well go over and check on Joe while we are on this side of town."

Dr. Hayden congratulated them once more, and everyone went his or her different way.

Charlene said, "Do you mind going back to see Joe with me? Or do you need to get back to work?

He responded, "Are you kidding me? Of course, I will go with you. Come on."

Charlene said in a jokingly threatening way, "He better be in a good mood today or else!"

Sean laughed aloud at the thought of this pint-sized girl giving Joe what for.

She said, "When do we talk to Pastor Jones? Do you do that? Our parents? Who?"

Sean squeezed her hand and said, "One way or another, we will do it. It will get done." And he gave her that priceless smile.

By now they had entered the rehabilitation center where Joe lived. When they walked into the room, Joe was indeed surprised to see them, especially to see Sean again so soon.

Charlene greeted him much the same way as she had in the past, but she said, "I understand someone has already beat me to sharing our good news."

Joe responded, "Yes, he just left a few minutes ago, stepping mighty high. Man! How can one guy be so cotton-pickin' lucky? Congratulations, Charlene. He really is a great guy. And I must say he didn't do half bad himself."

"Sean, did you tell him about our scholarships?" Charlene inquired.

Sean said, "No, I was too excited about our engagement. Did you show Joe your ring? No, I didn't tell him that part. You tell him."

By now Joe said, "Well, for Pete's sake, somebody tell me something!"

Charlene stuck out her hand for him to see her ring, and all the while she was talking about them receiving four-year scholarships to Johns Hopkins University.

Joe said, "Wait a minute. That university is not around these parts. I don't remember reading about that school in the vocational catalogues. Where are you two going?"

Charlene laughed and said, "No, you wouldn't likely read about it in a vocational catalog. Anyway, Johns Hopkins University is in Maryland. We plan to be married before we leave for school. We are hoping to be married in the first part of August. We just wanted our friends to know before they hear it from someone else."

Sean said, "Say, I need to get to work. My boss will send out a search party, looking for me, if I don't get down there pretty quickly."

They said goodbye to Joe and went down the hallway to the parking lot, where their vehicles were parked.

Sean saw Charlene to her car, and then they went their separate ways.

On Sunday morning, Jerimiah, Margaret, Sean, Mr. and Mrs. Stevenson, Sean, and Charlene were all seated on the same pew. Sean leaned over and whispered in Charlene's ear, "I went by the pastor's home yesterday, told him about our engagement, and said we would like him to do our wedding. He said to let him know as soon as we have a firm date, and he will put it on his calendar in ink."

The choir was singing, and people were still being seated. Once the singing stopped, Pastor Jones stood behind the pulpit and said, "Our community has suffered a lot during the past few years. Now there are many signs of hope for the future. There have been many changes in our community. New businesses are coming into town. The dam will be completed in a couple of years. We have a class of seniors graduating this coming week. Several of our students are going away to college, including our own Sean and Charlene. They will be attending Johns Hopkins University on four-year premed scholarships. We want to congratulate them on those achievements." Clapping erupted from the congregation.

"And, ladies and gentlemen, it is my privileged to announce their engagement." The congregation sighed; there were oohs and ahhs, and then began the uproar of clapping hands. "They will be marrying before leaving for school out east. I am thankful that on this day I can stand before this congregation and say our community has something extra special to celebrate. I have not received word about the other students who will be attending colleges; nor have I heard where they will be attending. When I have that information, I will happily share their good news with you in order that we may celebrate with them as we are celebrating with Sean and Charlene. I am sure that if Sean and Charlene were to stand before you today, they would both say these past four years have been grueling and hard. They have worked hard, helping their parents make ends meet during hard times.

"They have never given up hope on their dreams of one day going to college. I, along with their parents, were invited to the high school this week when Sean and Charlene were notified of their four-year scholarships. Hope is returning to Wilsonville.

"Folks, God has allowed us to be tested almost to the breaking point these past four years. Now we are beginning to see the fruits of being faithful and diligent, continuing to work hard, and keeping our eyes on our goals. These two-young people have taught me many lessons these four years as I have watched them give up their childhood and step into an adult world of many pains and uncertainties.

"God rewards those who are faithful, just, and true. That doesn't mean there won't be hard and trying times. It does mean He will be walking beside us when we do not know where to turn or what to do. We cry ourselves to sleep many nights when we see friends suffering, feeling helpless on how to help them.

"Then, when good things come back into our lives, it is like a cool, fresh breeze. Like an ice-cold drink of water on a hot, sweltering day. God has sent us a cool, refreshing breeze or a refreshing, cold drink of water. His word refreshes us. We must keep our eyes on Him as He keeps His eyes on us. If He even knows how many hairs are on our heads—yes, I know, for some of us He doesn't have to count very far—then He even knows when a little sparrow falls. He knows and cares for all of us. Thank God for His faithfulness."

His sermon continued, and soon the last song was sung and the last prayer said.

Jerimiah said, "Let's go to Tom's restaurant. The check is on me. We can resume our conversation from last night. There are so many plans to bring together." He turned to Sean's parents and asked whether they would ride with him and Margaret.

Then he added, "I'm sure these kids would rather drive their own vehicle. We will see you kids over there."

Charlene gave Jerimiah a big hug and said, "We will see you there."

The parents were in deep conversation all the way to the restaurant. They discussed how best to help the "kids" while they were in college and yet stay out of their way.

Again, Jerimiah suggested, "What do you think of us splitting the cost for a one- or two-bedroom apartment for them near the university? Charlene said her daddy will send her a monthly allowance to help with expenses."

Richard said, "Maybe we can all form a convoy to move them into the apartment and help get them settled in. But that means they will need to go early and locate housing before school starts."

Jerimiah said, "Remember, freshman orientation will be held sometime in August. Ladies, I hate to break the news to you, but we may have to move the wedding date back a week or two to make it all fit. First thing tomorrow, I will make some phone calls to the university and get a better feel for time lines. I'll check with some of the lawyers who are from the East Coast and may have some experience with Baltimore. I will put my secretary on the housing project. I will see what kind of information I can learn. Be prepared to hear from us probably more often than you would like.

"Off-campus housing will be cheaper. I'll let you know what we can learn. It may be that Charlene's dad may want to chip in on the apartment too. I know he is doing a lot right now—her car payment and insurance, gas money, and then an allowance. I don't want to stretch him, or any of us, too thin."

Richard said, "Nell and I married right out of high school. Neither of us went to college. Therefore, you are better prepared to make those inquiries than we are. Thank you for doing that."

Soon they were pulling into the parking lot of the restaurant. Charlene and Sean parked right next to them. When they entered the restaurant, they were seated in an area where they could talk freely without disturbing anyone. After orders had been placed and the conversation resumed, Tom Jackson came in to greet them.

He said, "Jerimiah, how are you connected to these kids?"

Jerimiah said, "I recently married Charlene's mother. I believe you met our kids Saturday night. This is Richard and Nell Stevenson, Sean's parents."

Tom said, "So that is why I have not seen you in here in a long time. That explains everything! Did the kids give you my cards and tell you about my offer?"

"Yes, they did give us your card. We are still discussing many options. Our heads are spinning with so much happening so quickly," Richard replied.

Tom asked, "How large of a wedding party are you expecting?"

"There will only be four attendants, with the rest of the wedding party making about fourteen, I think," Margaret replied. "We will be happy to hear your offer. However, please understand that we are planning to look at several options."

Tom said, "Sure. I will make up some suggested menus and prices, and you can have that for comparisons. Thank you for giving me a chance to offer my services."

By then, servers were carrying trays of wonderful food to the table. It wasn't long before talking drew to a minimum as happy customers settled in on a delightful Sunday meal.

Tom said, "I will check back with you to see if there is anything we can get for you. Enjoy your lunch."

After he had moved from their area, Nell said, "I have an idea I would like to throw out for discussion. What do you think of barbecued brisket and chicken, potato salad, baked beans, coleslaw, French bread, iced tea, and lemonade? If the weather is nice, we can have it outdoors. We could have pies and cakes for dessert. What do you think?"

Charlene said, "That sounds so good! Sean and I don't want to put a financial burden on you guys. I think it would be perfect. But that is simply my opinion. What does someone else have to say?"

Margaret said, "I like your idea. I can help you. We could borrow folding tables and chairs from the church. We could help you with cooking the meat. Jerimiah is getting quite good with his new barbecue pit, which is built in on the patio. We will gladly help however you want us too. You just tell us how best to help. We don't want to be in the way."

From there the conversation went on as plans began to fall into place. There would be many more similar conversations in the few short weeks left before the wedding. But first there was a graduation that had to be the focal point this week. There were two days left of school for seniors, the graduation rehearsal, and all the prep for the actual graduation. Caps and gowns had been ordered several weeks ago.

Chapter 16

✦✦✦

G raduation day arrived. The little town was abuzz with excitement. Charlene's dad was seated with Margaret, Jerimiah, Nell, and Richard. The graduating seniors marched onto the stage in an orderly fashion, each dressed in a graduation robe and cap. There were five empty seats with a bouquet of flowers on each, representing the five students who had died in the car accident. Parents would be given their sons' and daughters' diplomas posthumously.

Then Mayor Dyer gave the graduation speech. He gave a very moving and challenging talk that seemed to be directed at each one of the seated seniors. He acknowledged the five empty chairs of deceased students.

After he completed his speech, the superintendent of Wilsonville Independent School District, Dr. Ramsey announced the names of the valedictorian and salutatorian.

He said, "There has been a lot of excitement in the lives of these students—so much so that they didn't tell their parents about this part. They wanted it to be a surprise. These two have been in competition for the top grade since kindergarten. Sean Stevenson is valedictorian, and Charlene Jamison is salutation. There is only one-one-hundredth of a point separating these two GPAs. Folks, in my book that is essentially a tie. You should have been in the office when these grades point averages were being tabulated. At times, I thought we would have to call in the school district's CPA to obtain the final and accurate count."

Laughter from the crowd could be heard.

"Representatives from Johns Hopkins University, who are here today, will be personally awarding these scholarships. I know I am stealing Principal Taylor's thunder, but Wilsonville, we have much to celebrate with this graduating class. I will turn the mic over to Principal Taylor."

Taking the mic, he said, "Counselor Merriman and I worked with these students as they prepared their speeches. We didn't send the speech-writing exercise home as homework as in previous years. Other students must have wondered why these two were sent to the principal's office so often. But Sean and Charlene wanted this surprise to be a gift to their hard-working parents, who have supported them through the years." The crowd clapped.

"Sean and Charlene wanted this to be a surprise for their parents. These two students have received four-year premed scholarships to Johns Hopkins University. And one other item I might mention in passing—they have a wedding planned for this summer. Other than that, nothing is going on in their lives. Please join me in congratulating these two students." The crowd stood to their feet, applauding loudly.

"Ms. Merriman will announce the other scholarships being awarded to other well- deserving students right after the valedictorian and salutatorian have given their speeches."

And so, a most memorable graduation ceremony continued until the last student had received his or her diplomas and the last honor had been bestowed on deserving students.

Chapter 17

❖❖❖

After graduation was over, Jerimiah, true to his word, set to work making inquiries about the freshman orientation, housing, and so forth, even starting immediately after the graduation ceremony. He had managed to talk with the representatives from Johns Hopkins University immediately after the scholarship presentation and ceremony had ended. He and Margaret invited them out to dinner along with Nell and Richard.

Over a late dinner, the representatives gave the parents a lot of good information on which avenues to pursue regarding housing and which areas to avoid, including which areas were close to the university.

Jerimiah said, "I will have my administrative assistant begin immediately to follow up on this information. You have been most helpful. May we contact you in the future if we have additional questions?"

Business cards were exchanged.

Nell and Margaret began planning for their children's wedding. Charlene asked her mother whether it was all right to ask Sean's mom to go with them when they went shopping for a wedding dress, and the answer was a resounding yes.

The three women set a Saturday to go shopping. Since both moms worked five days a week, the only time they could be together was on a Saturday. It took two Saturdays of walking store to store, even in towns nearby, trying on dresses and looking and looking, before they found the perfect dress.

Nell said, "Honey, you look like Cinderella, and you are even more beautiful in that dress. Sean may faint when he sees you coming down the aisle. I'll tell Pastor Jones to have smelling salts in his pocket just in case."

Even the wedding consultant, who was assisting them, burst into laughter.

Now to find shoes, and then that item could be checked off the to-do list. The consultant also helped them find appropriate mother-of-the-bride and mother-of-the-groom dresses and shoes. Three very happy women went home with their purchases, each wanting to please the men in their lives.

After Jerimiah had received the information he needed about orientation, enrollment, and so forth, the parents could finally place a firm date in ink on the calendar for the wedding to take place. August ninth would be the date. Now to call the pastor, reserve the gazebo, call the bakery, notify the attendants, make arrangements with the city for use of the park, and make a host of other arrangements.

Jerimiah told Margaret, "Each thing leads to another. It is like pulling a string, and things began to unravel. Each thing is tied to the next. And you do not know what is next until you complete one thing that leads to yet another. Margaret, I've never been involved in anything this exciting. I want everything to go perfectly for our little princess. Do you think we should have Nell and Richard over and see how they are faring with all this activity?"

Thus, another evening of planning was arranged between the two families.

Richard said, "I've talked with Pastor Jones. He said there are several women in the church who want to help with the wedding reception. They have offered to make punch, cakes, and cookies—which leads to another discussion. Where can we hold the reception? If the wedding is at City Park, the church recreation hall is much too small for the number of people who want to attend. Other than the high school gym, there isn't a place here in town large enough to accommodate the size of the crowd the pastor is expecting. The other thing we discussed was to use the church reception hall and have tables and chairs set up under the trees in the church yard. I kind of like that idea. It would be pretty neat to hang white paper wedding bells and streamers from the large branches in the giant trees. This idea would make it a community affair. Seems to me that the gym is so impersonal. Several of the church ladies have said that they will take care of punch and keep plates of cookies and servings of cake replenished. And men of the church have offered to set up and take down tables and chairs, decorate, or help in any way they can. If we plan to go that direction, it would pull the community into our celebration. It is good to see the community pull together and celebrate once more like we used to."

Nell said, "Richard, that is beautiful!" Turning to Jerimiah and Margaret, she said, "What do you think?" Just as she asked that question, Sean and Charlene walked through the door.

Sean said, "What do we think of what?"

The parents repeated all that had been discussed this evening, including what Richard had just said. Sean said, "You go, Dad! I like your idea. What about you, Charlene?"

She responded, "When they were talking, I could just see those white bells hanging from giant limbs on the trees and swaying while white streamers fluttered about in the breeze. It sounds lovely. I like the idea. You guys have some fantastic ideas. Thank you."

Nell said, "I was thinking of how best to do the invitations to cut down costs. Why don't we put an invitation in the paper, inviting people to attend the wedding in the park? For out-of-town family and friends, we could send a formal invitation."

Charlene said, "I brought in the mail earlier today. There was a letter from Daddy. He sent two hundred dollars to be used wherever I might be needing it and that was before he knows about the wedding. Has the cake been ordered? Or what about flowers? The check is on the counter in the kitchen. I have been thinking about matron of honor and bridesmaid bouquets. How about white daisies or white carnations that have blue ribbons, matching the dresses, streaming from their bouquets? I am still thinking about my own bouquet. Haven't come up with anything for sure, but I'm thinking strongly of white roses with blue ribbons. Is it appropriate for the bride to throw another bouquet rather than her bouquet? I really want to keep my own bouquet. But I will do whatever you think is appropriate. I was wondering about putting my bouquet in a nice vase on the table with the cake and having another one, not so expensive, to throw. Is that silly thinking?"

Jerimiah said, "Sean, you have to get a garter for Charlene's leg."

Sean said, "A garter? Why does she need a garter? I've never been to very many weddings, and I sure don't remember anything about a garter."

Richard explained the custom that some couples do and said, "Sean, if you rather skip that custom, that is just fine. One thing we want you kids to understand is this is *your* wedding. Charlene, whatever you want to do with your bouquet, I would say it is appropriate. It is your wedding."

Margaret said, "This week we need to get invitations mailed out. Nell, if you and Richard can get a list of out-of-town family and friends you want to invite, then Charlene can begin working on those, unless you prefer to write them yourself. I have already begun a list for Jerimiah and me. I am thinking an invitation per each office building should be sufficient for our fellow workers to feel included. I am not sure how you want it handled for your office, Jerimiah. Just give us names and addresses."

Nell replied, "We have been thinking about that ever since the kids announced their engagement. I have begun a running list. Each time one of us thinks of someone, we write down their name. I have their names in my address book."

"Oh! I need an invitation for Dr. Hayden and the lab staff," Charlene exclaimed.

Margaret said, "Write it down."

Charlene said, "I will be working for Mrs. Samuelson on Monday, Wednesday, and Friday afternoons. Then on Tuesdays and Thursdays

I will continue to do lab work at the hospital for two more weeks. But the rest of the day I should be free to do whatever is needed."

Richard stood up and said, "We all have to be at work early in the morning, so we better be heading home. I think this has been a very productive evening. Flowers and cakes and passing the word on to the pastor, and we will soon have this wrapped up—that is, so long as nothing raises its ugly head. Jerimiah, does the city sound agreeable?"

Jerimiah said, "I am still working on some details. As soon as I have everything together, I will pass along the word." By then Nell and Richard were approaching the front door.

Sean said, "I need to go, too. I have to open up the store in the morning, so I have to be there early."

Everyone walked onto the front porch to watch the guests as they departed. However, Charlene escorted her handsome groom-to-be to his ol' truck, which had so much character.

She said, "I love this truck."

Sean said, "Hey, you are supposed to love *me*." They shared a quick good-night kiss, and he pulled away, driving along the driveway, down the hill, and out of sight.

Jerimiah continued working with the city. Unbeknown to his family, he had paid for a new coat of white paint and tiny white lights to outline the gazebo. Various repairs were made to the area around the structure, including a handicapped ramp installed at the back of the gazebo. The medical personnel should be able to move Joe's wheelchair up the ramp without great difficulty. Each parent was busy working with his or her individual assigned responsibilities. A beautiful wedding was soon well planned down to the last detail, including wedding rings and arrangements for a honeymoon suite to be reserved in a neighboring town.

Chapter 18

✦✦✦

August ninth arrived like a runaway train. Ready or not, the big day had arrived. The day came with the checking and rechecking of lists. The rehearsal dinner had been a huge success.

For the rehearsal dinner, the Stevensons had put out quite a spread. The food was delicious, and the rehearsal had gone off without a hitch. Now for the wedding to go off as well.

The weather was perfect—not too hot or cool, not rainy, just about perfect. The white lights were turned on for a seven o'clock wedding, with flowers lining the steps that entered the gazebo. Newspaper reporters from Wilsonville and neighboring towns were in position for good photographs, just so long as they didn't interfere with the wedding photographer. Pastor Jones and Sean were in their positions. Joe had been helped into the gazebo, and Charlie Samson was in his position. An electric piano was playing; the sound system had been tested and was working just fine. Many chairs borrowed from neighborhood churches had been set up around the front of the gazebo and along each side of the sidewalk. A huge number of people were standing at the back of seated guests and along the sides of the gazebo.

Mrs. Samuelson came down the sidewalk and was assisted up to her position by her son-in-law. Next Mary Sue James assumed her position. Children from the church scattered flower pedals along the sidewalk, while older children handed little packages wrapped in blue nylon net fabric, tied with blue ribbon, to all the seated guests. The packets were filled with bird seed to be thrown instead of rice.

The musician began playing "The Wedding March." The crowd stood to their feet and turned to see the father of the bride and the stepfather of the bride escort Charlene down the sidewalk, up the steps, and into the hands of her groom.

Sean couldn't take his eyes off his beautiful bride as she came down the sidewalk and up the steps to be with him forever.

The ceremony began. To this day neither Sean nor Charlene remembered a word Pastor Jones said except for "You may now kiss your bride."

Chapter 19

✦✦✦

The young couple moved to Baltimore, Maryland, to begin their college careers. Fortunately, they had a couple of weeks to get settled into an apartment before classes began. They quickly acclimated themselves to the city and nearby shopping centers. And they discovered the shortest routes to and from classes.

Charlene continued her habit of letter writing. Those who frequently received her neatly penned letters, besides their parents, included Charlene's dad, Mrs. Samuelson, and Pastor Jones. Occasionally she dropped a note to Dr. Hayden and the lab team.

The time flew by with a steady schedule of classes. The first year, the second year, and now the third year flew by. They both completed all premed classes that were required, and they gained lab experience.

The young couple managed to go home for Christmas and Easter holidays, but generally they stayed in Baltimore.

Early July before their senior year approached, a message from Margaret said Mrs. Samuelson was seriously ill, and her recovery didn't look good. On the very night the letter was received, they received a phone call saying she had, in fact, passed away. Sean and Charlene told Margaret they would be there. Hurriedly, the two packed, locked up their apartment, and headed for Wilsonville. They drove straight through. Two exhausted young people drove into Wilsonville. They stopped to see Sean's parents and then drove on to Charlene's home, where they would spend the night.

The next day, they went to visit friends. This included Dr. Hayden and the lab crew, plus a stop to see Pastor Jones. He asked about their plans while in town.

Sean said, "At seven o'clock this evening, we want to go to the gazebo. That place has special significance for us. Tell us about what all is new in Wilsonville. It appears that several new businesses have come into town. I saw that *my* drugstore has been bought out by Walgreens."

Pastor Jones said, "The dam has been completed for over a year. Several hotel chains have begun buildings along the lake. A new highway is being built around that area. Several recreation businesses have opened. The town is gradually recovering. I contend that it will be better than ever."

"It is so good to see you again, Pastor Jones," inserted Charlene. "We need to go to the hospital to visit friends there. We will see you again before we leave for Baltimore."

Sean said, "I wonder where Joe is and what he is doing. Maybe Dr. Hayden can tell us."

Charlene stuck her head into the lab doorway to see whom she might recognize.

The supervisor saw her and called out to everyone, "Charlene is here!" The lab team pulled off gloves and protective eye wear, and went over to say hello. They visited for a few minutes, then began to drift back to their stations to resume their work. Charlene said goodbye to them and went to see Dr. Hayden. He was at one of the nurses' stations. They had a pleasant but brief exchange.

Sean asked, "What happened to Joe? Where is he these days?"

Dr. Hayden said, "Joe has had a really rough time. He has been battling depression, as is often the case with lone survivors. He is still receiving help. He is making some progress. He is mobile. He walks with a cane, which really hurts his ego. Maybe someday he can dispense with that thing.

"I'm changing the subject on you. Your wedding and reception were a turning point for the morale of this town. The light began to return in the eyes of people that weekend. It was as if hope had finally returned. It was a beautiful ceremony and reception."

Charlene said, "To be honest with you, I do not remember a single word the preacher said except, 'You may now kiss your bride.'"

Sean chuckled and nodded. He said, "We better move along. We don't want to keep you away from your patients. Good to see you again."

After they exited the hospital building, Sean said, "Do you remember where Joe lived?"

Charlene answered, "Not really. I know he lived in an area of town that had a higher income than my side of town, which was the poorest area." She stopped, drew in a deep breath, and said, "It feels strange to not be going to visit Mrs. Samuelson. I miss her. She was the closest person I had to a grandmother. I loved that lady. She was such an encourager. I hope I can be that for a student or someone someday."

Sean suggested, "Let's go have lunch at Tom's restaurant. I wonder if that place is still there. I wonder if he is still there."

As they were going out the hospital door, they met Mary Sue. Hugs and hellos were exchanged.

Charlene asked what she was doing there. She said, "I work here. I am a licensed vocational nurse. This is a great place to work."

Sean asked, "Do you know where Joe lives?"

She replied, "Yes, are you sure you want to go there? He is really into drinking and is a mess. Dr. Hayden has been trying so hard to get him dried out and on to the right path. It is like he has given up. He is so depressed."

She told them where he lived, then said, "I must get back to work. Good to see you two."

Sean said, "It is nearing lunchtime. Let's go get something to eat and then go find Joe on the way home. Aren't we supposed to have supper with my folks tonight? And to spend the night with them? This can get complicated, can't it? I want to see both sets of parents as much as we can. Really pulls me in two. What happens when we have kids?"

Charlene laughed and said, "We can leave the kids with one set of parents and go spend the night with the other set." They both laughed at that silly thought.

Some things were a constant. Tom's restaurant was just the same as it had been almost four years ago. When they went through the door, Sean saw him, walked across the room, and said, "Mr. Jackson, I am sure you do not remember us. We are Sean and Charlene Stevenson."

Before he could say another word, Tom said, "Of course you are. How is life in Baltimore? Say now, your wedding and reception were something out of a fairy-tale book. Whoever planned that did an excellent job. And I understand your mother put on a barbecue spread to top them all. What a clever idea. Your wedding was the best thing to happen to Wilsonville in a long time. The town had something to celebrate, and hope has been restored. But I think I said that once upon a time."

Sean said, "We are starving and heard this is the place to be."

Tom said, "Come this way. Let me grab you a couple of menus."

After they had consumed their meal, they said goodbye to Tom and went back to Wilsonville to see whether they could locate Joe. When they drove into the driveway of his home and started up the sidewalk, Joe called out to them. He was in a lounge chair under a shade tree. He said, "Can I help you?"

Sean said, "I am looking for an ornery guy by the name of Joe. Do you know where I can find him?"

Joe sat bolt upright, knocking over beer cans and said, "Sean? Is that you? Charlene? What are you two doing here? Please, please come over here and join me."

Charlene said, "Joe, how are you? How are things going for you?"

Joe rubbed his hands across his face and said, "You two are the last persons I can lie to. You two know me too well. I am not worth anything. I do not have any purpose. Why am I left here? Why couldn't it have been me that is gone?"

Charlene said, "For one thing, you made a promise to me. You promised that you would get out of the hospital, go to campuses, and tell kids your story. You said you wanted to change the lives of other people and not allow them to go down your path. Well, I am here to hold you to it. When is your first scheduled talk? What school? I will want to know all about it. Remember?"

"Oh man! Charlene, you are hard on a guy. You don't have any sympathy."

"Joe, it is not sympathy you are needing right now. It is for you to get up off your heinie, be a man, and meet your responsibilities. Do you want me to write letters to the schools and schedule your talks?"

By now he was standing and not using the cane. He walked over to her and said, "You would do that too."

She said, "Yes, if that is what it takes, you can bet your sweet life I will write those letters, giving them your name, address and phone number for them to contact. Now do you want me to do that, or are you going to step up to the plate and follow through?"

"Sean, rescue me!"

Backing up, shaking his head, Sean held up both hands in a defensive way. "No, Joe, you are on your own. This is not my battle. She may be pint sized, but she is mighty. Just give up and do what you promised."

By now Joe was laughing. He said, "You two really know how to challenge a guy. I promise, *re-promise* that I will do it. No, no need for you to write those letters and make the contacts. I will do that myself. I promise. Or I know you will appear on my doorstep again."

The friends visited for several minutes, then said their goodbyes. After they were seated in the car, Charlene wrote down Joe's address. A follow-up letter in a few weeks might not hurt anything.

The first night back in Wilsonville was spent with Charlene's parents. They tried to divide the time equally between parents. The next night, Sean and Charlene went over to his home. They would be there, waiting, when his parents came home from work. Charlene said, "I could start dinner if I knew what your mom had planned to serve. Want to call her? It might help her out."

He called his mother, who told him exactly what she had planned to serve. There was a casserole ready to go in the oven. They could make a salad and heat garlic bread. She was picking up a pie at the bakery. Iced tea was already made and in the refrigerator. They quickly set the table, made the salad, and had the casserole in the oven with garlic bread on standby.

Both parents arrived within minutes of each other. They had a nice, hot meal waiting for them when they entered the house.

During the meal, the conversation varied over many topics. Then Sean's dad said, "Tonight will be the fireworks display at ten o'clock. Are you planning to attend?"

Sean and Charlene looked at each other with blank looks on their faces. Then Sean exclaimed, "This is the Fourth of July. Of course! Sure, we want to go see that. We will go early. We want to drop by the gazebo at seven o'clock just for old time's sake. I just want to see what it looks like at that time when I'm not looking for a certain beautiful bride to come walking down the sidewalk, heading toward me."

Charlene started removing dirty dishes from the table, and Mrs. Stevenson began cutting the pie and placing delicious servings of chocolate cream pie before her family.

After the kitchen was cleaned up and things were put away, Sean said, "We will take the blankets for us to sit on and go ahead. We will use them to save a good place on the lawn because there will be a very large crowd."

Sean's dad said. "Good idea. We will be there before eight o'clock. See you then. That way we can visit some more before the fireworks starts."

Soon the foursome was seated together near the gazebo. Sean had picked out a good place to watch the fireworks display. Their earlier conversations continued as they waited for the show to commence. Someone kept walking around and Charlene looked to see who it was or what might be the problem. She looked straight up into the face of James. She said, "James what are you doing here? Where is your lady friend? Is she here with you?"

He said, "We are twenty-one, and this is the Fourth of July, and that is the gazebo. Did you forget? Anyway, I do not have a lady friend. We broke up again ages ago, this time for good."

Sean, Nell, and Richard were all interested in this exchange.

The fireworks began right at ten o'clock making conversation rather difficult. Charlene was leaning against Sean, as she watched the first rockets shoot toward the sky.

Fire trucks were stationed around the park in case there was a fire or accident. This year it seemed that the fireworks were far more elaborate than in recent years. Some children covered their ears and looked up at the brilliant colors and designs, while others hid their faces against their mothers, not daring to look at the noisy explosions

In order to be heard, Charlene began speaking louder, "Yes, as a matter of fact, I *had* forgotten that promise we made as eighth-graders. Anyway, you moved away and didn't want anything to do with me. So, I moved on too."

In all the confusion and loudness, Sean stood up, shook hands with James, and said, "Good to see you, James. When did you get into town? Where are you going to college?"

James said, "I drove in today. Looks like things are changing for the better in Wilsonville. I am glad to see it. I am going to the University of Wyoming. Where are you two going?"

Sean responded, "Charlene and I are attending Johns Hopkins University, premed program. We drove in yesterday."

James said, "You drove in yesterday—together?"

Sean responded, "Sure, why wouldn't we travel together? We have been married almost four years."

James said, "Oh, I didn't know. Congratulations. But I must ask, which of you had the higher GPA?"

"The superintendent said it was a virtual tie, but I did edge her out by one-one-hundredth of a point. I think she let me have that one-one-hundredth of a point to smooth my ego."

Charlene said, "Don't you believe it! He just caught me in a weak moment. Anyway, I like a *powerful, strong* man." Everyone laughed at that image.

As in times gone by, the threesome resumed their friendly banter. Suddenly, Richard said, "We remember you. Where did you and your parents move to? Awe, wait! I remember. Idaho! Come and sit down and tell us about your life out west."

James thanked Mr. and Mrs. Stevenson and joined them. Then he turned to Charlene and said, "Since you forgot about our eighth-grade promise, what, might I ask, brought you back to this fair city on this particular weekend?"

Charlene said, "Do you remember Mrs. Samuelson, my wonderful friend? She passed away. We are here for her funeral."

James said, "I am sorry to hear that. She seemed like a nice lady."

Charlene said, "She was. She was the closest thing to a grandmother I ever had. I loved her very much."

The conversations continued until late, and most of the people had gone home when Mr. and Mrs. Stevenson said, "I think it is time to call it a night."

Sean said, "Us too. After the funeral tomorrow, we will head back to Baltimore. It was good to see you, James. Drive carefully as you go on your way." With that, they all said good night and parted.

Charlene took Sean by the hand and said, "That was weird. When they were here for Joyce's funeral, he had a beauty queen—Miss Rodeo, 'who excited him'—and he didn't want to hear from me again. So, I wrote him off. Wonder where she is and why he came back to Wilsonville. But I don't want to know bad enough to ask."

Sean laughed and gave her a hug. He said, "You are one spunky little piece of dynamite. I love you. Please don't ever write me off."

She turned, looping her arm through his, adoringly looked up at him and that infectious grin, and said, "You big, handsome galoot, how could anyone ever write you off? I love you too."

The next day was Mrs. Samuelson's funeral. The pastor's talk was centered on a "Life Well Lived." Charlene thought, *How appropriate. I hope someday someone will say that about me.*

After the funeral was over, Sean and Charlene gave hugs and kisses to their parents and loaded their vehicle to head back to Baltimore. Just as they were driving away, she saw James leaning against a tree, watching them drive down the street and out of sight.

Chapter 20

✦✦✦

Their senior year at Johns Hopkins seemed to go by in a blur. Not only was their schedule intense, but they also contacted various hospitals and research centers about grants. Some of the department heads helped them with grant writing. They explained that they were a married couple and wanted to be considered a research team. They were doing extra labs and making sure all premed prerequisites were checked off before graduation.

Late in their fourth year, under advisement from their professors, they applied to many. doctoral programs in medical research. They hoped they could go as a packaged deal to med school, though that wasn't necessarily the general application process. But they were already becoming well known as a hopeful genetic and cancer research team. They had both completed their undergraduate work with 4.0 GPAs. They mailed out résumés and transcripts to numerous medical research schools, but deep down they knew there were hundreds of other deserving students with excellent records who also wanted good schools to accept them. Certainly, with records like theirs, graduate schools would hopefully take a second look at them. Through their four years as undergraduates, they had both worked part-time at hospital labs. Also, for extra money at the university, they tutored students in math and science. They were well known to the staff and faculty and were highly respected and received many awards and letters of recommendations. They both had an unquenchable thirst for learning.

Each day they rushed back to their apartment to check the mail to see whether there were any responses from the schools where they had applied and from their requests for grants.

Days and then weeks went by. They were beginning to think they would need to start applying for jobs to financially support themselves until they could hear something from perspective colleges. They talked with their professor friends, asking them for advice for the next step.

They continued to tutor students in math and science during the summer sessions. The summer semesters were shorter and more intense; therefore, many students needed extra help.

Just before the second summer session began, they received word that the University of Texas Graduate School of Biomedical Sciences at M. D. Anderson in Houston, Texas, had accepted them and that they both had received substantial grants. Now an excited wave and flutter of activity began. First order of business was to contact their parents, including Charlene's dad, and share the good news.

Back in Wilsonville, two sets of parents seemed to burst with excitement as they shared the good news with anyone who would listen. Jerimiah told everyone that "our kids" were going to med school.

Margaret said, "I know one of the first persons Charlene would have told would have been Mrs. Samuelson. I will call Mrs. Jacobson this evening and tell her. She can tell the superintendent, the principal, and guidance counselor. There is someone else Charlene is concerned about. That is Joe. She wants to know if Joe has signed up to speak at the high school. I will find out if he has kept his promise. Oh yes, we must let Dr. Hayden know."

Nell dropped by the church to let Pastor Jones know the good news. He said, "This good news deserves a phone call to the local paper. What do you think? They will want to know about these two hometown kids. That will be a good article for the hometown folks to read."

Richard posted a note on the bulletin board, saying, "Our kids are going to med school."

A few minutes after Charlene had called her dad with their good news, he called back, saying, "I have not taken my vacation this year. I will be happy to take a week or ten days off and help you move to Houston—that is, if you want me to. Let me know. I can be of help to you in finding housing. After you check in with the main campus, they can tell you the most convenient places to live. It is a real puzzle when you get downtown Houston into that medical complex. That area is unbelievable … a real nightmare for out-of-towners. Let me hear what you think of my idea. My truck will pull a U-Haul trailer, and I can carry things in the bed of the truck, too, if necessary. I will be waiting to hear, so let me know as soon as you can. I will need to give my boss a few days of notice that I am planning to take vacation time."

Sean and Charlene discussed the offer and happily agreed; of course, they would welcome his generous offer to help them move. Immediately Charlene called him back and said, "We would be so happy for you to help us move and to find a place to live. Houston is so huge! Sure not like Wilsonville! From what you have said, I think Wilsonville could fit into the medical complex. Do you think a week or ten days are too soon for your boss to okay your vacation time? Let us know what he says after you talk with him. In the meantime, we will begin to pack. Amazing what you can accumulate in four years. Sean says we will have a garage sale or give away as much as we can. Love you. Thanks again."

The next phone call was to Sean's parents. Sean told them to pass along the word to Jerimiah and Margaret that George would be helping them move to Houston. His truck could pull a small U-Haul trailer and carry things in the bed of the truck. "Along with our two vehicles, we should have enough space to carry everything we do not sell or give away."

Chapter 21

+ + +

M oving day arrived. George backed the pickup with trailer attached as close to the apartment as possible. Neighbors began carrying out boxes, a TV, a few pieces of furniture, and so forth. With so much help, the job was completed in no time. George stayed at the trailer positioning boxes, strapping down furniture, and finding spaces for oddly shaped objects while the young people did all the heavy lifting.

While the guys carried boxes, the ladies helped by running a vacuum cleaner, wiping down the shower, and doing other jobs so the apartment would be welcoming to the next residents. College students form a close camaraderie with fellow students and are frequently more than willing to help one another.

Charlene had packed an ice chest with cold cuts, cheese, chips, cold drinks, brownies, cookies, and various snacks for the long trip ahead. She made up a small ice chest and snack box for her dad to have in his truck, containing things he would enjoy. She had contacted the highway department, gotten two sets of travel maps, and marked the route they would be traveling along with rest stops and picnic areas. George had gotten two handheld radios so they could communicate with one another.

As the vehicles left the apartment, they waved to all their helpful neighbors, and the journey to Houston began. Sean towed Charlene's "little blue car" behind his pickup with character, and the convoy was lined up with George in the lead. The trip would be about 1,455 miles before weary travelers would arrive at their destination. The journey would take them across eight or nine states and through many miles of beautiful, scenic countryside. They had decided they would drive eight- to ten-hour days, depending on road and weather conditions.

After a long, hard journey, they pulled into the sprawling city limits of Houston. George led them to a neighborhood he thought would be most convenient for them. It was in the Meyerland neighborhood, where many med students lived and not far from the medical complex. There were several apartment buildings in the area.

George stopped in front of the office of an apartment complex. Several students were in the office when he entered. They were very interested in Sean and Charlene's academic pursuits and welcomed them to the community. They gave names and addresses of apartment buildings with vacancies.

George said, "You guys are better than an apartment locator and a lot cheaper." He thanked them for their help, and they drove to the next building.

Soon they looked at a two-bedroom, furnished apartment. It was nothing fancy, but it was adequate.

George said to the manager, "It is in bad need of a coat of paint." The manager nodded in agreement. George said, "If we buy the paint and paint the apartment, will you give us a discount on the first month's rent? I've done a lot of carpentry and painting, so I know how much it will cost to have a professional painter come in and paint this apartment."

The two haggled, quibbled, and discussed the price of paint and labor. Eventually George was victorious in getting a reduction of the first month's rent. They signed a lease agreement and asked for directions to the nearest hardware and paint store, grocery store, and shopping mall.

Sean unhitched Charlene's car from the pickup, and the threesome went paint shopping. After a stop at a McDonald's for a quick lunch, they returned to the apartment with painting supplies. The three of them were soon busy painting the walls with an egg-shell white paint. When the job was finished, the apartment looked bright, clean, and fresh.

The apartment manager stopped by to check their progress. He was so impressed that he said, "I can put you on the payroll, and you can be my maintenance guy. You do very nice work."

George said, "Thank you, but I have a job over in Georgia that I need to get back to, but I will keep your offer in mind."

They carried in boxes from George's pickup. The trailer would have to wait until the next day to be unpacked. They located boxes containing sheets for the two beds and bath towels. The day had been long and tiring.

Sean went to a nearby Pizza Hut and brought back pizzas and bread sticks plus drinks. The hungry and tired travelers were thankful for a meal and the promise of a bed waiting to receive weary bodies.

Early the next morning, the threesome began unloading the U-Hall trailer. George said, "At this point I am very happy that this is a small trailer and that you don't have a lot of stuff like a piano or a sleeper sofa. It is a long way up to the second floor on these old legs. I wish some of those college kids in Baltimore would drop by."

At last the final box was inside the apartment. Now Sean and Charlene would have to do the rest of the work.

George grabbed a quick shower, put on clean clothes, and said he needed to head back to Georgia. They thanked him over and over for all his help. Sean said, "Now you know where we live. You must come back sometime for a visit."

George said, "By the way, I will continue to send money each month to help with expenses. I am so proud of you two!"

There were hugs and handshakes, and then the two stood, waving to George as he pulled away from the curb. He would drop off the U-Haul trailer at a nearby business.

When Sean and Charlene turned to go up the stairs, Charlene said, "I miss him already."

Sean put his arm around her, and the two went trudging back up the stairs to put their new home in order. Boxes were stacked on the counter and along the wall in the kitchen. Boxes were in the bedrooms and bathroom. The place looked like a disaster zone. But in a couple of days, everything would be in its place. The phone must be installed, and several other things needed to be taken care of before classes began.

They both needed to complete enrollment for the fall semester and pick up their schedules. Also, they needed to familiarize themselves with the campus and where classes would be held, plus determine how much time to allow to be at class on time.

Within the next few days, the apartment was put in order, all paper work was completed at school, and the long, grueling doctoral experience would begin. According to their schedules, several of their classes would be together, but some were separate.

As Charlene dug deeper into cancer research, the more intense her classes became.

Sean had about the same story with genetics. At times, they felt like ships passing in the night. They were thrilled when Christmas break arrived. Both were exhausted. They planned to take two or three days just to rest and reconnect with each other; then they planned to go to Wilsonville for a few days. They felt a need to be with family.

Chapter 22

♦♦♦

Christmas break was exactly what the two kids needed. Once home with family and friends, the two began to unwind somewhat from the toils of the last few months. Their plans were to be in Wilsonville until after Christmas, then to head back to Houston. They tried to divide the time equally between parents and have time together with both sets.

Once while at Margaret and Jerimiah's house, Margaret said, "Jerimiah and I have been talking about what to do with the little house in town. We have been renting the house out and sending the rent money to you each month. With all the expenses of medical school, we are wondering if the rent check will be adequate along with what George is doing, including Nell and Richard's share.

Jerimiah was thinking of contacting a financial advisor through his firm to see what the best avenue was regarding help with med school expenses. "Well-kept rental properties are in short supply. We may do some upgrades and increase the price of rent. We are all trying to think of ways to help you so that you can concentrate on your studies and not worry about finances."

Jerimiah said, "We are sure thankful for the grant money. The two fields you two have chosen touch right on the areas of life where so many people are suffering. And here's some fatherly advice: whatever you do, make time for each other. Schedule time each week *just for the other person*. Keep your love for each other first and foremost in your lives."

Charlene said, "Jerimiah, thank you. We will remember that. As we get our feet on the ground a little more and figure things out, we may be able to work some to help with finances. Right now, we are just trying to figure out the system, the right ways of doing things and staying focused on the expectations for us at school."

The days of the visit at home flew by. Soon it was time to return to Houston. They took a few days of vacation time and met George at a halfway point between Wilsonville and Georgia. They visited with him a couple of days, then returned to the apartment.

They checked in to their respective departments at M. D. Anderson. Their advisers assigned them to work in labs until classes resumed.

Once classes resumed, again there were just brief encounters with one another. Sometimes they were scheduled to do labs together, or if lucky, they had class time together.

Charlene didn't feel well. She wasn't sick, just felt "bum," as she called it. Sean was very concerned about her. He mentioned this issue to one of his professors. He told Sean to take her to one of the doctors, who frequently checked on the health of med students. The appointment was made.

When Charlene came out of the examining room, Sean was waiting for her. He said, "What is wrong? Could they find a cause for you not feeling well?"

She looked at him and smiled. "Do you call pregnancy a *cause*?"

His eyes bulged out, and he said, "What? Pregnancy? You mean, we are going to have a baby?" Then he laughed aloud, grabbed her up, and swung her around. Everyone in the waiting room was watching. He said, "We are going to have a baby! We may have a special present for our August anniversary!"

They laughed with him and clapped loudly when he said, "I can't wait to tell our parents they are going to be grandparents."

At the end of the day, after the last class and lab, two tired but happy people were at home in their apartment, making phone calls and telling five happy parents they were going to be grandparents. Once again, the news spread across Wilsonville like a whirlwind.

Overall, Charlene felt good. Prenatal vitamins helped a lot. She was very healthy, and the baby's development was right on target.

The next months would be labs and classes, research, papers, labs, and classes. Two expectant parents asked other students how they managed as parents. Many answers came back. Very young babies even went to some classes. Husbands and wives traded off class times and labs so one parent would have the infant while the other was in class. Some even had a parent living with them, caring for the infant. They were assured, "It will work out! Don't worry."

Sean and Charlene were even more in love now than before, if that was even possible. They would squeeze in a time to meet in a park for a picnic. They used many creative approaches to keep in contact.

Soon it was time for the little one to be born. All five parents were contacted when labor pains began. Soon a tiny baby boy made his appearance. Grandparents arrived shortly after the birth of their grandson.

Sean looked at the tiny infant as if he had discovered a pot of gold. He was awestruck as he looked at the perfect, little person. He said, "I didn't know I could experience this level of love for someone so tiny." Charlene lay on her bed, watching him hold his son. It was the most amazing experience of her life.

They had discussed many names for their child. Sean asked, "Charlene, what do you think of us naming him after my granddaddy? His name was Richard Joseph Stevenson. Grand Daddy Stevenson is the reason I am in genetic research. He was a marvelous man. He was to me what Mrs. Samuelson was to you, only on a deeper level because I got to have him longer."

Therefore, the little boy was now named after a well-loved grandfather.

Soon the five grandparents arrived at the maternity ward to greet their newborn grandson. They were once again amazed at the miracle of birth as they stared into the face of this precious child.

The new grandparents stayed in a nearby hotel. They were at the apartment as much as possible, caring for Charlene, Sean, and tiny Richard Joseph. His five grandparents bought food for the small refrigerator freezer. They brought in boxes of diapers. They tried to do as much as they could to help during the few days they could be in town. They took turns holding the baby when he cried so Charlene could get some much-needed rest.

Sean was just bursting out with pride over his tiny son. There was no way possible to wipe the smile off his handsome face. He didn't want to leave Charlene for a second and desired to be near his son. It was a happy family time. Someone had a camera in his or her hands, always ready for the next little squirm or stretch, grunt, or smile. For the time the parents were there, Charlene didn't need to lift a finger if she didn't want to.

Soon time came for the parents to go their respective ways. Charlene and Sean once again stood, waving goodbye to those they loved dearly.

By the time classes resumed, Sean and Charlene had a routine worked out. They had decided that the one who had class would have the baby in a sling on his or her chest while the other was in labs. Gradually it all worked out just as their peers said it would.

Weeks turned into months, and baby Richard continued to grow. By the end of the semester, he was placed in a carrier on the chest of either Sean or Charlene. He seldom cried or squawked out during classes. The professors considered him a member of the class.

One day toward the end of the semester, Richard was a little fussy.

The professor approached Charlene and said, "May I?" He took the baby, who stopped fussing immediately and smiled broadly. The professor continued teaching the class.

Charlene and Sean had been discussing options for child care.

Some of their friend traded off babysitting with one another. But again, that became pretty involved with trying to mesh schedules of classes, labs, and so forth. They thought about neighbors who might be willing to babysit.

Then one day they received a letter from George.

Dear Sean, Charlene, and baby Richard,

My company is expanding and will have a branch in Houston. I want to run an idea past you. You two have several more years of med school, and someone needs to take care of my grandson. If I accept the position at the Houston plant, what do you think of me keeping Richard while you two are in class? There are three shifts, and I can pretty much set my own schedule. Let me know if you think this might be doable.

Love,
Grandpa George

Sean and Charlene danced around the room, celebrating like two teenagers. Sean said, "I wonder whether he would like to share an apartment with us. We are about to outgrow this one. I'm calling him right now."

George picked up the phone on the fourth ring. He was delighted to hear from his son-in-law. Sean told him they would gladly accept his offer to be a grandpa nanny.

George got a belly laugh out of that title. Then he said, "Sean, I was thinking of something else. I'll mention it to you, and you can run it by Charlene. What do you think of us renting a larger apartment?"

Sean responded, "Seriously? I can't believe that you ask that. That is what we were discussing. We were wondering if you would consider such an adventure."

Charlene leaned in close to Sean so she could hear the conversation, which continued for several minutes. The basic details were worked out.

George said, "I will be moving to Houston in about six weeks. That should give us enough time to locate a suitable dwelling." With that the phone calls ended. Three happy adults began planning for the next move.

Sean checked with the apartment manager to see whether there were any large, four-bedroom apartments in his building. The answer was no, but he knew some other people he could check with. Then he asked, "Have you considered renting a house? For about the same price or a little more, you can lease a house and still be fairly close to the hospital complex. Think about it."

Chapter 23

✦✦✦

A house was located with a fenced-in yard for little Richard to play in. Soon everyone was settled into a routine of sorts. Sean and Charlene's hours were often hectic and long. More than once Sean and Charlene told George he was an answer to prayers.

The next two and a half years would be grueling and after that residency, plus a fellowship for their specialty, if they chose that route. Yes, George was a true blessing, and he and that little boy were the best of buddies. Everywhere George went, he had a little tagalong walking in his shadow.

When everyone's schedules meshed and all could be home for a meal at the same time, it was a time of celebration. Sean and Charlene still tried to go to Wilsonville for a few days during the holidays, and the four grandparents tried to come for a visit when schedules would work.

The time went by in a flash. In many ways, it seemed like it had taken forever, but at last Sean and Charlene graduated at the top of their classes. Charlene would do her residency at M. D. Anderson in the cancer wing. Sean accepted a residency at Houston Methodist DeBakey Heart & Vascular Research Center to continue his focus on genetics. His goal was to further his training in his specialty of genetics into heart issues that appear to be inherited. Eventually he might pursue a fellowship, but for now, first things first. At last he and Charlene were receiving paychecks.

When their first paychecks arrived, Charlene said to Sean, "I want to send some money to the food bank at our church. They helped Mother and me when we were in trouble and deeply needed the help. I want to help someone else."

And many years ago, when she and her mother had had only one can of tuna, a half jar of peanut butter, and a few slices of bread in the pantry, she'd promised Pastor Jones that one day she would pay back every can and pound of food they had received. She wrote Pastor Jones a letter.

Dear Pastor Jones:

Many years ago, you helped Mother and me when we were in need. I promised you then that one day when I had a job, I would repay the food pantry. I thank you for your love and support during those awful days and times. It was people like you, our church family, Mrs. Samuelson, and others who made the times not as bad as they could have been. This is the first of more checks to come. May God continue to bless you, our church family, and Wilsonville. Enclosed is a check to be donated to the food pantry.

Most sincerely yours,
Dr. Charlene Stevenson

Chapter 24

+♦+

The young couple fell into a new schedule of sorts. There were more and more times when the family was together for an outing or just to celebrate being together. There were always laughter and practical jokes pulled on one another.

Once George laughed so hard at them that he said, "You two remind me of a couple of puppies who have been in a cage and have been set free."

Of course, little Richard was always in the middle of anything happening.

One night at the dinner table, Charlene said, "What would Grandpa Nanny say if he had *two* little charges to watch after?"

Everyone was so excited about the news that even little Richard, with a big, infectious smile like his daddy's, clapped his small hands and said, "Yeah," though he didn't realize his world would never be the same again with a new, little person to take away some of his glory. By the time the new baby arrived, little Richard would be entering prekindergarten.

Phone calls were made to the rest of the grandparents. Then celebration began anew in Wilsonville. These were happy, blissful days.

Weeks and months sped by, and time approached for the new arrival. Charlene waited until she could bear the pain no longer before she went to the hospital. A tiny baby girl soon made her appearance.

Sean said, "She may be tiny, but she has lungs that are well developed, and she sounds like she is in control of the nursery already. She seems to have an air of determination. I wonder who she might take after!"

The tiny pink bundle of energy was named Margaret Nell. Maggie soon had her daddy wrapped around her little finger. She was his little princess. When he was home, little Maggie was in his arms. Richard loved her and was super gentle and tender with his tiny sister.

When Maggie was three, another baby boy joined the family. He was named George Michael Stevenson, after Grandpa Nanny George and Sean's father. They called him Mike. And another little boy was born close after him. He was Sean Jerimiah Stevenson.

Once again, the family had more than outgrown their home. Sean and Charlene purchased a large home in Spring, Texas, a Houston suburb. Sean took Charlene in his arms, kissing her, and said, "It is not a white house on a high hill overlooking a beautiful valley, but it is a lovely home."

It was large enough to accommodate all of them, including Grandpa Nanny George, with room to spare. Also, there was a maid's quarters over the four-car garage. Grandpa Nanny George had extra help since Charlene and Sean employed a housekeeper/driver to help with doing chores around such a busy household and transporting children to various events.

The years sped by with small children turning into middle-size children and then teenagers. There were swimming classes and T-ball and later basketball, tennis, various clubs, and—horror of horrors—driving lessons. One or both parents attended as many sports or school events as possible. There was always something happening at the Stevenson's home.

Charlene and Sean's individual practices and research projects continued. Each were frequent guest speakers in their chosen fields. Their comfortable life had been achieved.

The year they celebrated their twenty-fifth anniversary, they were each working on their individual research projects when Charlene received a phone call.

The voice on the other end of the phone said, "Sean was found slumped over in the lab. He's in the ER. Come quickly."

With her heart racing, Charlene hurried to Methodist Hospital, where Sean was being treated. One of the doctors on her team drove her to the hospital.

She was immediately rushed to his bedside. His ashen color, the oxygen mask, and the concerned faces of the cardiovascular team hovering over him told her all she needed to know. She knew instantly he was in serious trouble.

The head of the cardiovascular team said, "He has had a massive heart attack. It doesn't look good. All I can say is, the next few hours will tell the story. As soon as we can move him, we will be putting him into ICU. You may want to notify the family to come as soon as possible."

A doctor escorted her and her teammate to a private room, where she could make the necessary phone calls to five parents. She was thankful the maid was there to care for the children. George was at work. She contacted each one, then went back to be with Sean.

They moved her out of the space where they were working on Sean. She wept, saying to her doctor teammate, "He is my rock. He is the kindest and most gentle, loving man I have ever known. I don't know how I can possibly live without him. I have known him almost my entire life. He was my first and only boyfriend."

The hospital chaplain entered the room and began to minister to her. He prayed with her. By now George had arrived with all four children.

He said, "Margaret, Jerimiah, Richard, and Nell are on the way. It is over seven hundred miles. If they drive straight through, that will be about ten to twelve hours of hard driving."

Charlene went back across the hall to see whether any changes for the good had occurred. She asked, "May I speak to him?"

They allowed her to hold his hand and tell him he was in good hands and all the things a doctor would say to another doctor. Then she said, "Sean, I love you. Keep fighting for us."

The doctors gently moved her back across the hallway. They understood she wanted to be there by his side but not right now.

Several members of her medical team arrived to be with her. The children were allowed to see their daddy. They stood in shock, looking at their big, strong father in a hospital bed with so many machines and tubes attached to him. They had never seen him ill a day in his life. Charlene said, "The doctors are taking care of him."

George said, "I'm calling the housekeeper to come take the children home. This is too stressful for them to be here right now." A nurse directed him to a phone.

A member of the cardiovascular staff said, "We are moving him to ICU. He will be on life support. We will try to see if giving the heart a little rest will help."

Charlene thought she knew what that meant. She turned to her daddy's arms and cried.

The older children reached to comfort the younger ones, and they all had tears in their eyes as they fought back the burning-hot tears that would soon come.

Several minutes later, the housekeeper arrived to take the children home. Charlene hugged and kissed each of them, from the biggest to the smallest, and told them she loved them.

Charlene followed the cardiovascular team as they moved Sean into ICU. She stayed by his side, ever watching the monitors and knowing fully what each reading was telling her.

The head of the cardiovascular team came in and told her, "You need to go get something to eat. We will give you a pager. I will be staying here with him while you are away."

Hesitantly, she left her vigil and grabbed something to eat. Whatever it was, it was filling. Her taste buds didn't register pleasure or displeasure. She had no recollection as to what she had eaten. Her mind was upstairs in a sterile room with all sorts of machines and tubes attached to the love of her life.

The four parents took turns driving all night. They arrived just before noon the next day. The five parents, Charlene, and the children were allowed to see Sean one last time before he was unplugged from all the machines. And he slipped away into eternity.

Chapter 25

◆◆◆

Newspapers covered the story of Sean's death. The headlines read, "FOREMOST CARDIOVASCULAR RESEARCH DOCTOR DIED AT HOUSTON METHODIST DEBAKEY HEART & VASCULAR RESEARCH CENTER, HOUSTON, TEXAS." They were careful to say he was working on a genetic breakthrough to fight heart attacks. The story continued, "He was waging a war on the genetic defect that causes heart attacks running in his family and in many others. He was in research because his grandfather had died of a heart attack. He wanted to be the one to find a breakthrough in finding a cure."

In Wilsonville, the gazebo had black bows attached to all sides. Word of Sean's passing was on the lips of everyone.

Sean's body was returned to Wilsonville for burial.

The next weeks, months were a struggle. Grandpa George was the strength everyone turned to. The children talked with him for hours.

Charlene continued with her treatment and research of cancer. She could console children and adults. She often thought, *I can comfort them, but why can't I treat my own broken heart?*

Soon Richard, who had his daddy's infectious smile, graduated from high school. Then Nell finished middle school. The other two were growing up so quickly. She looked at her beautiful family, and tears welled in her eyes. She thought, *Sean didn't get to see his children grow up.*

The next five years went by somehow. The family tried to have the same fun they used to, but it wasn't as enjoyable as when Sean had been there. He had been the biggest kid of the bunch. They all missed him.

Gradually a routine was established. Charlene was at the research center one day when one of the research assistants came in and said, "There is someone to see you."

She replied, "To see *me*? Really? Who is it?" She walked down the hallway and entered a waiting room. There stood James. Shocked, she said, "James, is that you? What are you doing here?"

He said, "I have been in Texas, doing a lecture series on equine science at Bryan-College Station and asked about a research team by the name of Stevenson. That was when I learned that Sean had passed away. I wanted to say how sorry I am for your loss."

She responded, "Thank you. We are getting along. My father lives with us, and that helps a lot."

You said, "Us?"

She said, "Why yes, we have four children. One is graduating from Texas A&M this fall. Then we have three more in the lineup."

He laughed and said, "Wow! Four. Boys? Girls? Mix?"

She smiled. "Yes, four. Three boys and one girl. The girl may remind you of someone. She is the woman in charge. She is super organized and has a plan." They both laughed.

Then Charlene said, "What about you? Married? Kids?"

He looked at her seriously and said, "No, I never married. I let *the one* get away from me. I've never met anyone else like her."

Charlene said, "I am sorry. Where are my manners? Would you like to sit down? Would you like something to drink?"

James responded, "I distinctly remember hearing those same words some time ago in our history. And I would like to pick up where we were, there on your front porch so many years ago, Charlene. I am not going away ever again. I foolishly let you go once but never again."

Printed in the United States
By Bookmasters